Cordelia and the Whale

Michelle Nelson-Schmidt

Foreword by

Asha de Vos, Ph.D.

MNS PRESS / PERDIDO KEY

Michelle Nelson-Schmidt/MNS PRESS
13430 Gulf Beach HWY # 132
Perdido Key, Florida 32507
www.MNScreative.com

Author: Michelle Nelson-Schmidt
Title: Cordelia and the Whale/Michelle Nelson-Schmidt
Description: First edition. | Florida: MNS PRESS, 2018. | Summary: A magical blue whale, Beatrice, helps a young girl, Cordelia discover her own magical abilities and powers through self-belief and connection to her community.

Identifiers: ISBN 978-1-7326942-0-0 (Hardcover) | ISBN 978-1-7326942-1-7 (Paperback) | ISBN 978-1-7326942-2-4 (Ebook)

Text Copyright ©Michelle Nelson-Schmidt, 2018

Illustration Copyright ©Michelle Nelson-Schmidt, 2018

Book Cover Design by Melinda Mesina.

Editor: Emma D, Dryden, drydenbks LLC

Ordering Information: Special discounts are available on quantity purchases by corporations, associations, and others. For details, contact the publisher at the address above.

Perdido Key / Michelle Nelson-Schmidt — First Edition

Printed in the United States of America

Cordelia and
the Whale

Lukas,

Soar!

♡

michelle Nelson-
Schmidt

*For Sophia Jane, the first child to hear
this book in its entirety - until now.
May she continue to bless those who knew and
loved her with her everlasting joyful spirit.*

*And for her Mom, Erin - one of the most beautiful
people I've ever had the pleasure of knowing.*

Contents

★ x ★

Foreword

When Michelle originally reached out to me to write this foreword, I was pleasantly surprised. She was committed to supporting Oceanswell, my organization, regardless of whether or not I accepted. She had clearly read about what we do and believed in it, and of course just the mention of a blue whale got me curious. Michelle lives in the US and I live on a tropical island on the other side of our planet. After reading some of her other children's books, I was curious to know what magical adventure she had woven that involved two of my favourite things—blue whales and my island home. Suffice to say, I was not disappointed.

No sooner had I started reading this wonderful little book when I was drawn right in. Not merely because Beatrice is a magical blue whale (and we all know blue whales are magical!), but because this book is more than just a story of a little girl and her magical friend. In fact, it echoes many of the things I believe in very strongly, messages I like to share, and in some ways I felt like I was reading my own thoughts.

In a world where people, and particularly kids, are driven by external validation, in a world where you are not cool if you don't fit a stereotype, this book reminds us all that *self-belief is one of the most important tools in our tool boxes. Cordelia was not—by definition—cool. She got bullied by the kids in school, people thought she was weird, but in the end, it was the magic of self-belief that changed that perception. She felt empowered by a few simple words, that helped her to rise as a leader, and even brought a town together. In the end, she could not be defeated.*

If more kids were empowered to be themselves, celebrated for who they are rather than what the world thinks they should be, and were encouraged to believe they can do anything they set their minds and hearts to, we would be nurturing a generation of true leaders who can be the change we need for this world.

Perhaps everyone needs their own Beatrice—I for one am sure glad I have a whole population of them!

-Asha.

Dr. Asha de Vos

Founder, Oceanswell
Sri Lanka's First Marine Conservation
Research & Education Organization
www.oceanswell.org / info@oceanswell.org
Senior Advisor, Oceana
Pew Fellow in Marine Conservation
National Geographic Explorer
TED Fellow
WEF Young Global Leader

Cordelia and the Whale

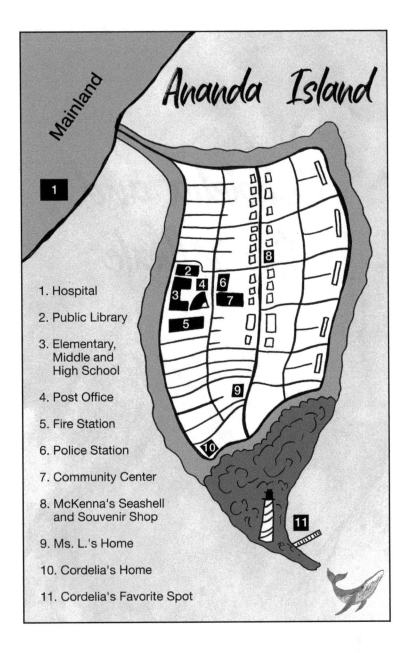

Ananda Island

Mainland

1. Hospital

2. Public Library

3. Elementary, Middle and High School

4. Post Office

5. Fire Station

6. Police Station

7. Community Center

8. McKenna's Seashell and Souvenir Shop

9. Ms. L.'s Home

10. Cordelia's Home

11. Cordelia's Favorite Spot

There's an island where magic lives and breathes.
It's not a vaudeville sideshow of tricks and illusions. It's a real island filled with real people and with the magic of the universe. It wasn't always that way—and it won't stay that way if everything continues as it should. The people there will be spreading the magic far and wide—one day.

Right now, though, they're all still learning. Learning from a young girl named Cordelia—who learned from a blue whale named Beatrice.

This is their story.

1

Cordelia

It was summer vacation and the normally sleepy little island where Cordelia lived was jam-packed with tourists. People were everywhere on Ananda Island, enjoying the vacations they'd saved up for the entire year. For nine months out of the year, there were no lines, no crowds, no traffic, no people practically—but after Memorial Day came? Everywhere you looked—lots and lots of people filled up the island, and filled up McKenna's Seashell and Souvenir Shop, the beach store Cordelia's parents owned.

Cordelia's parents made most of their money for the year in those three months, so she didn't see them all that much during the summers—unless she went to hang out at the store.

Cordelia's older sister, Janey, worked at McKenna's too, but Mom and Dad didn't want their youngest to work yet. They wanted Cordelia to have the kind of childhood they'd had. Her parents had grown up on the island. They'd grown up playing together, and had what they called a "magical childhood." Cordelia had heard that phrase so much growing up she'd started asking Mom and Dad where their wands and fairy dust were if everything had been so magical.

When Cordelia said something smart like that, Mom used her full name. "Cordelia Joy, watch your mouth young lady."

Actually, Cordelia did know how lucky she was to live on Ananda island. She loved her home. She loved that normally there were hardly any people around. Cordelia was not what you'd call a people person. She was more of a loner and she was okay with that—she preferred it that way.

But Cordelia's parents wanted her to have "grand childhood adventures" and "magical childhood experiences." *We still live in a place where neighbors know and watch out for each other, where everyone knows everyone else's names, where people don't have to lock the doors at night and kids can stay out until after dusk,* and *blah, blah, blah...* Cordelia and Janey had heard all of that about a million times. At least.

"Cordelia," Dad would say, "you're eleven years old! Work will be waiting for you for the rest of your life. Go out and be eleven! Have fun with your friends!"

Which was all well and good. Except for the part about friends.

Cordelia didn't have many of those.

Well, there was Maddy Mason. Cordelia had sat with her at lunch this past year. But that was only because Cordelia preferred books to people and Maddy felt the same way. Cordelia had tried talking to her once, around November, but Maddy had just glared at Cordelia then put her nose right back into her book.

So, Cordelia guessed, Maddy didn't really count as a friend after all.

Nope. No friends. Cordelia didn't really mind it that way. She was fine with no friends.

Absolutely fine.

2

Family

"**W**hat are you up to today, Cordelia?" Mom asked on the second day of summer vacation. Mom was simultaneously scrambling eggs, frying bacon, getting a cup of coffee for Dad, and checking her email. Cordelia was always amazed at how much Mom could do all at once while never getting frazzled or mixing up any of it. Cordelia always had to concentrate hard on one thing at a time, making sure to focus on a single task until it was done. Her brain didn't seem to work like Mom's did.

"I was thinking I'd come by the store and help you unpack the new stuff," Cordelia said, spreading strawberry jam on her toast.

She could tell Mom was frowning even though her back was to her. "Cordelia...."

"Mom, geez," Janey said. "If she wants to come help, let

her help! There's nothing wrong with having a good work ethic. Besides, I like having her there." Janey winked at her sister.

Cordelia adored Janey. She was seventeen and a senior in high school. And she was everything Cordelia was not. She was outgoing and popular, but not in that mean girl, cliquey kind of way. While Cordelia could remember everything she ever read and could tell you about any subject she read about in detail, Janey had the ability to just...understand people. She could talk to people as if they'd been friends for years—even if they'd just met. Cordelia tried at school, but she never knew the right thing to say. She either didn't talk enough or she talked so much that kids rolled their eyes and walked away. Janey always knew what to say and exactly how to say it. Everyone on the island loved her.

She was smart, athletic, and beautiful on top of it. Janey looked just like Mom and had long straight brown hair that looked perfect even when she'd just woken up. As she smiled back at her sister, Cordelia absentmindedly fingered the unruly red curls she tried to keep controlled in ponytails. Whenever summer came, her hair just got bigger and bigger with the rising humidity, and Cordelia had to admit, though she did adore Janey, she *was* jealous of her big sister's sleek ponytail.

"You know how your father and I feel about that, Janey. No working at the store until Cordelia's thirteen. We want you both to have childhoods. We live in a place where that's still possible. You know, it's not everywhere kids can run around..."

"Mom's right, Cord," Janey interrupted. "Go play today."

Cordelia silently thanked her sister for stopping Mom's "magical childhood" lecture. She knew Janey would let her in McKenna's back door later to hide somewhere with her drawing pad or a book.

"Okay, okay. I will, I will." She didn't dare tell her parents she really had no friends.

Cordelia knew she wasn't the same as other kids. They thought she was weird—and told her so regularly. But Cordelia didn't mind sitting alone with her thoughts while everyone else was talking over each other. She could do without all that noise. She'd never quite felt like she fit in. She never got the jokes her classmates cracked that made the whole class—and sometimes even the teacher—laugh, while she sat there not knowing what was so funny.

She was just as happy sitting and thinking as she drew for hours in her sketchbook, got lost in a good book, or researched some new subject she found fascinating. Her most favorite thing to do was sit on the old pier after it got dark and stare at the stars and the moon. Cordelia liked to think about things. *I think...I think maybe I'm just a "wonderer." I don't mind that at all. Why does that have to make me weird?*

"Cord? *Cordiiiiii?* Did you hear me?"

"Sorry, Dad, what?"

"Always lost in that head of yours." He tugged one of Cordelia's curls. "I said please clean up the kitchen before you go out, okay?" Then he grabbed Mom's phone from her hand.

"Jonathan James! I was texting the delivery company about today's order!" Mom protested as Dad began twirling her. He dipped her to the imaginary music in his head and kissed her.

"Oh, yuck," said Janey, fake-retching.

"What, a man can't get a morning dance in with his beautiful wife before work?" Dad twirled her back to the spot she'd been standing and returned her phone. "I swear you get more beautiful every day, Maxine Lorraine! I am one lucky man!"

Mom glared.

"I love you...Max," Dad said quickly and kissed her on the nose.

Mom hated her given name. She'd been going by "Max" since forever and Dad normally went by "JJ" unless he was in trouble with Mom.

Cordelia and Janey made a few more retching noises, but it was all in fun. They loved how in love their parents were. Mom and Dad had been married for what seemed like ages, because they'd been friends since they were kids and had started dating in college. They were total opposites. Mom was organized, tidy, and a bit on the serious side, while Dad was...a bit of a mess to be honest—and an eternal optimist. There wasn't a situation he couldn't turn into a positive. It often drove Mom a little crazy, but they were best friends.

"Got it," Cordelia said. "Clean the kitchen. No problem."

Dad grabbed his coffee, kissed Mom again, kissed Cordelia and Janey on top of their heads, and headed out the door. "See you two at the store later! You go have fun, Cordelia! That's an order!" They could hear Dad's whistling as he walked down the street.

Cordelia cleared her plate. "Don't forget sunscreen

and bug spray," Mom said. "Otherwise you'll burn and get eaten alive!"

"Got it. Don't burn. Don't get eaten. Love you, Mom. I'm going to get dressed. I'll clean the kitchen before I leave."

Janey stood up. "Love you, Squirt." Then she mouthed, *See you later* before asking, "Hey, Mom, can I drive?"

"Janey, the store's half a mile away. We're walking."

"But I need to practice! All my friends have cars and I barely drive! You have to let me grow up! I'm going to be in college next year. What am I going to do then?"

Mom sighed. "You won't need a car at college."

"*Mommmmm....*"

"Okay, okay. No need to whine. I'll let you take the car out after work. Deal?"

"Deal!" Janey grinned and bounced out the door, her perfect ponytail bouncing along with her.

Mom turned to Cordelia. "Stop growing up so fast, okay, kid? I can hardly stand it."

"I'll try." Mom kissed her head in the exact same spot Dad had and left to catch up with Janey.

Cordelia wished she could freeze time. She didn't want to imagine Janey gone off to college any more than Mom and Dad did.

Why do things have to change? Why can't things just stay how they are?

3

Ms. L.

Cordelia got dressed, loaded the dishwasher, packed herself a quick lunch for later that day, wiped down the counters, and was just about to head outside when she heard a meow. "Kalispell! Where have you been, kitty? I haven't seen you in days!" The fluffy gray cat wove its way through Cordelia's legs meowing, demanding to be fed.

"Well, come home every once in a while and we'll feed you, silly!" The cat had shown up as a kitten one day and adopted the family. Mom swore they were *not* taking in the cat, but eventually the little kitten had worked her way into Mom's heart. She'd had Dad put in a cat door and they chose the name Kalispell because it was where Dad had proposed to Mom during a cross country road trip one summer.

Even though Kalispell was the family cat, she'd immediately chosen Cordelia as her favorite person. She followed Cordelia around from room to room, settling on her lap or at her feet, and she slept at the foot of her bed. Cordelia had felt an immediate connection with the kitten too. It was as if they just...belonged together somehow. And when Kalispell wasn't around for a few days, Cordelia always knew the cat was fine—she didn't know how she knew. She just did.

"What do you do when you're gone?" Cordelia shook kibble into Kalispell's bowl. The cat looked at her without blinking, and Cordelia could swear Kalispell was trying to answer her. She crouched down and stroked her silky fur. "I would love to know what goes on inside your cat brain. How fun would it be if we could talk to each other?" The cat purred in response. Cordelia stood up, grabbed her tote bag, and opened the door. "See ya later, alligator!" Kalispell briefly looked up from her bowl as if to say goodbye, then went back to eating.

Cordelia walked down the street. It was already hot and steamy even though it wasn't even ten o'clock. It was too early to sneak into McKenna's. She'd wait until the tourists were all over the place. Once the store got busy, her parents would hardly have a moment to leave the register and Cordelia could slip in unnoticed.

"Hello, Cordelia, dear! Where are you off to today?"

her neighbor Ms. L. called from her porch. Cordelia shielded her eyes as she walked over to the tall, elderly woman. Ms. L. was a retired school teacher who'd moved to the island after she finally decided the New Jersey winters were just too much for her. She loved children, and retirement didn't stop her from being with them. She volunteered so much at the Ananda Island Elementary School, that she was adored equally by the teachers and children. Cordelia had known Ms. L. her entire life; she was practically a grandmother to her and Janey. She was one of the few people besides her family members who Cordelia truly felt comfortable around. Ms. L. always made her feel special.

Ms. L.'s whole name was Ms. Roselynn Liebowitz, but when she arrived on the island, she'd told everyone to call her Ms. L., pronounced "Miz-elle" because that was easier for kids to say.

"Not sure, Ms. L. Just wandering. Wandering and wondering. I'll probably find something to draw or just read a book." Cordelia motioned to her tote that was stuffed with her art supplies, lunch, and dog-eared copies of her favorite books.

"Come sit with me a bit, dear. I could use the company. Unless you're in a hurry?"

Cordelia skipped up the steps and sat down on a chair with a bright yellow and white cushion.

"Tea? Coffee? Water?"

Cordelia liked that Ms. L. offered her the same choices she would to an adult. "Maybe just some water. Thank you."

Ms. L. poured a glass of ice water from a pitcher on a tray in front of her. There were several glasses, coffee mugs, and teacups. Cordelia wasn't the only guest who would be visiting her friendly neighbor's porch today.

"Can I ask you something?" Cordelia wiped cool drops of condensation from the glass that were dripping onto her leg.

"It's why I invited you up, dear! Of course!" Ms. L. smiled and handed Cordelia a fancy embroidered napkin.

"You've known a lot of kids in your life, thousands and thousands probably, right?"

"At least. I taught for over fifty years. And truth be told, I'm not done. I just don't get paid for it anymore. I enjoy sharing knowledge; I just can't help myself!"

"I want to know about kids...like me. Do we turn out okay?" Cordelia set her glass down and looked very seriously at her silver-haired friend.

"Kids like *you*?"

"You know what I mean. I know I'm not normal. I'm not like Janey or any of the other kids at school. They all think I'm weird. I know I'm different. I don't mind being by myself...I don't mind being alone in my head. And then when I do talk, they make fun of me, too. I can't seem to figure out the rules that everyone else seems to know. So I'd rather be alone. It's easier. Mom and Dad, I know they worry. And if they knew I didn't really have any friends..." She studied an ant crawling next to her sneaker.

Ms. L. set her tea cup down. "Darling, first let's get this concept of 'normal' taken care of. There's simply no such thing as 'normal.' I've met many children through the years. And there's nothing wrong with *any* of you. We're not all alike, that's true. All our brains work a little bit differently. Some more differently than others—not wrong—just differently. And some of us—like you and like me, Cordelia, we just have so much going on in our brains. We think about so much, we wonder about so much, we're just so very entertained by everything in front of us, that we just...we just don't need that much more than our own thoughts. We're kindred spirits, Cordelia. Made of the same star stuff." Ms. L. tapped Cordelia's knee affectionately.

"The same star stuff," Cordelia exclaimed. "Do you think I'll be a teacher like you? I do like to explain things I learn about. Once I read it, I remember it forever."

"Maybe, maybe not. You've got plenty of time to decide what you want to do with your life. I have an eidetic memory like you—such fun to remember every sentence you've ever read, isn't it? I decided I wanted to learn as much as I could about all those wonders dancing around in my head and then share what I learned with as many children as I could. I much prefer the company of children to adults. Children listen for the truth, they keep their hearts open."

Ms. L. took a deep breath, shook her head, sipped her tea, then continued. "Never stop questioning and never stop learning, Cordelia. Never stop being willing to listen, learn, and admit that maybe...maybe you got something wrong, maybe you made a mistake. I'm eighty-two years old and I've gotten as many things wrong in my life as I've gotten right. Probably more!" Ms. L. laughed, her bright red lipstick making a perfect oval on her face.

"Ms. L.! I need to talk to you right now! Brian broke up with me!"

And suddenly Brittany Baker, a girl Cordelia recognized as one of Janey's classmates, was up on the porch, her eyes brimming with tears.

"Oh, darling! I'm so sorry. Come sit with us." Ms. L. motioned to the striped cushioned chair next to Cordelia. Brittany looked at Cordelia.

"I was just saying I have to go, Brittany. Sit here."

Relief washed over Brittany's face. "Oh. Okay. Thank you, Cordelia." She sat down and began sobbing.

Cordelia waved at Ms. L. as she walked down the steps. Cordelia thought about all those cups and glasses. *How many others will Ms. L. help today?*

There's no such thing as normal. There's nothing wrong with me.

Cordelia began to skip.

4

The Pier

Cordelia made her way through the brambles and brush along the path to the pier. It was at a part of the island where no one lived anymore. No one was allowed to build in the area and it had become a quiet sanctuary for lots of wild animals.

The pier and nearby lighthouse seemed to have been forgotten by most locals and they were unknown to vacationers. There wasn't an easy way to get to the small beach near it anymore thanks to all the overgrowth.

The pier was Cordelia's favorite place in the world. If she walked all the way to the end, all she could see was water. It stretched far out into the ocean with pilings that went down over forty feet deep. Just a few more feet from the end, Cordelia knew the ocean floor dropped to over a hundred feet deep.

The ocean made Cordelia certain she was part of something bigger than herself, and the very last thing she felt out here was alone.

Cordelia pulled a towel from her tote bag and set it on the hot pier. She sat cross-legged and watched a sailboat slowly make its way across the horizon.

She began slathering on sunscreen. *Mom's right, I'll fry like an egg if I don't use the spf 100. How is it Janey never, ever burns and has a perfect tan all summer long?* Cordelia sighed as she rubbed and rubbed the white lotion over her freckled knees and legs until it disappeared. Once she was finished, she pulled out her sketchbook and colored pencils and began to draw.

She was lost in her sketching, unaware of how much time had passed, when suddenly a giant gray and white pelican flew down and landed next to her, not three feet away.

"Hello, Charles. How are you today?" Cordelia asked the pelican.

The bird looked at her, and Cordelia could swear he nodded his head in greeting, then he turned back to the ocean.

"Searching for lunch, huh?" Charles just stared.

"Okay, I get it. You do your thing, I'll do mine." Cordelia began drawing the large sea bird as if it was the most normal thing in the world to be friends with a pelican.

Charles showed up almost every time Cordelia came out to the pier. She knew him from the section of missing and crumpled feathers in his tail. As she sketched, she wondered what kind of scuffle the bird had gotten into to lose those feathers. We *all have a story. What's yours, Charles?*

Just as she finished up the sketch, Charles abruptly soared into the air and across the water. Cordelia watched as he flew high in the air, banked left, then started diving towards the water at an incredible speed. Almost before Cordelia could register it all, the pelican dove, then popped back up with a fish hanging from its mouth.

"Bravo, Charles! Great job," Cordelia called. As if on cue, Charles performed the feat again. How amazing it must feel to be able to fly, dive, and spin across the sky like that. Cordelia watched him fly and dive over and over, getting his fill of fish.

Cordelia's pencil flew across the paper along with the bird, as she tried to capture his energy and acrobatics in her sketchbook. After one last dive, Charles made a large circle above Cordelia, then flew off along the coast, his belly full of breakfast.

-Cordelia McKenna

As Charles disappeared, Cordelia laid back on her towel, arms behind her head, and closed her eyes, the sun warming her face. She thought about the birds flying, the fish swimming, and wondered about all the experiences a human could never have and all the experiences animals could never have. Even though she couldn't actually talk with animals, Cordelia recognized she had some special connection with them—like with Kalispell and Charles. She swore they could understand her. Even the class goldfish, Mirabelle, seemed to swim towards her and watch her when she walked up to her bowl. She talked to Mirabelle every day when no one was around, or thought no one was around, but some kids in her class had noticed. "Geez Cordelia, do you try to be so weird or does it just come naturally? You can't talk to people, but you can talk to fish?" They had laughed and walked off, but she wished more than anything that it were true, wanted it to be true. Even without words, animals seemed to understand her a lot better than people did.

Cordelia's stomach growled. *What time is it?*

She peered up at the sun. She guessed it was well past lunchtime. She got up, stuffed everything into her tote, and walked back toward land.

Years ago, she'd asked Dad to help her set up a hammock between two trees on the shoreline near the pier. Dad loved the idea of creating a special, secret spot for Cordelia and readily agreed to help. They'd made a morning of it; picking the perfect spot, clearing away brush, setting up the hammock. Then they both got in and talked and spied objects in the clouds for hours.

She climbed in and unwrapped her peanut butter and jelly sandwich.

Cordelia ate the sandwich quickly, not realizing how hungry she was. She wolfed down the banana she brought, too. She pulled out one of her books. She'd read *Charlotte's Web* several times before and even though she knew everything that was going to happen, it still made her cry each time. She loved books that made her cry— even ones about spiders.

A few hours later, with the ocean breeze washing over her and the gentle sway of the hammock, Cordelia drifted off into a deep, dream-filled sleep.

Cordelia awoke and sat up abruptly. *How long have I been asleep?* The sun was setting and a few stars were already out. Cordelia had been dreaming she was flying across the water with Charles. It seemed so real she could still feel the wind across her face and the salty spray as she got close to the water. She still had the somersault sensation in her stomach as she flew from high up in the sky, turned alongside Charles, and dive-bombed toward the water. *What a great dream!*

Cordelia leaned back and closed her eyes. She kept replaying her dream in her head, committing the sensations to memory so it wouldn't fade away like the best dreams always seem to do.

When she opened her eyes again, it was even darker. More stars were out and the moon was rising.

She slapped at a sudden sting on her leg. *Oh, no!* Her legs were swollen with mosquito bites. She'd remembered the sunscreen but had forgotten the bug spray. *Oops. Oh well, what's done is done. Too late now.*

Cordelia climbed out of the hammock, stood up and stretched. She knew it was time to head home, but the stars were all calling to her.

What's another hour, right? Mom and Dad wanted her to have a magical childhood, and as far as Cordelia was concerned, there was nothing more magical than the ocean and a sky full of stars.

Cordelia walked back to the end of the pier, laid down, and stretched out on her stomach. She rested on her elbows to watch the sky light up in front of her, one star at a time.

The beauty and the vastness of the night sky almost made her dizzy. *Where's the beginning? Is there an end? Are there worlds out there just like ours? Could there be another eleven-year-old girl out there who loves animals and books more than people, looking up at the stars, feeling completely connected and all alone at exactly the same time, just like me?*

"I love you, stars. I love you, moon. I love you, ocean. Thank you for making me feel...okay," she whispered.

It was right at that moment, Beatrice knew the time had finally come.

5

Beatrice

eatrice knew she was taking a risk. Just getting so close to shore could cause so many problems.

A giant blue whale doesn't just swim up to a girl on a pier and start talking to her. Things like that don't usually go unnoticed.

Beatrice didn't trust most humans. They made terrible decisions most of the time—especially decisions that affected worlds they didn't know about—worlds they seemed to ignore for their own convenience. She could go on and on about the humans and her disappointment in them, but this moment wasn't about them. This moment was about one special girl—and why she was worth the risk. Worth any risk Beatrice could think of to finally connect with her.

When Beatrice thought of Cordelia, her huge heart swelled with love. Cordelia had a light inside of her so bright it had pulled Beatrice to her—like one of those lighthouses built to bring ships in safely to harbor on dark nights. Cordelia was Beatrice's lighthouse.

Except Beatrice didn't *see* Cordelia's light. She *felt* it. Beatrice was hundreds of miles away from the girl the first time Cordelia's energy and magic had connected with her own. As seasons passed and Beatrice migrated north and south, Cordelia's pull got stronger and more intense as she neared the island where Cordelia lived. It was a magnetic pull, a lulling, something calling to the giant blue whale that filled her with such joy, peace, and such a sense of—*homeness*? Yes, somehow Cordelia felt like *home* to Beatrice—as familiar to her as the deepest seas she'd ever swam; she knew Cordelia was the one she'd been meant to find.

It all started about eleven years ago when Cordelia was born. Which meant Cordelia was born with an extraordinary amount of magic. She was a human the Earth had not seen the likes of in centuries, and certainly not one Beatrice had felt or encountered in all her 904 years.

Beatrice was sure the humans would have noticed something different about Cordelia even when she was a baby. Probably said things like, *I know she's only a few weeks old, but look at her eyes—she has an old soul. She just looks like she knows things.*

But parents eventually forget about all that as the baby days turn to toddler days and then all those activities begin that humans like to keep themselves so very, very busy with. It's easy for parents to forget to keep 'seeing' their children.

Children could remind parents of the magic they themselves have long since forgotten, but children end up just as busy as the parents. That's when children begin to forget their magic, too. It fades away into a forgotten memory until some brief moment of magic happens. These moments of magic are usually called coincidence, luck, or a pleasant surprise.

When the magic happens, humans can feel it, they might even pause and wonder about it, feeling some spark of something familiar, a memory they can't quite put their finger on. Then the moment passes and they shrug it off, getting right back to their busy schedules, and the magic eventually gets forgotten for good.

But the magic was so strong with Cordelia that it was enough to make a giant blue whale swim from the other side of the world to find her. As the years passed and the magic didn't fade, but grew stronger, Beatrice's mission became clear. It was her job to show Cordelia who she was, teach her how to use the magic glowing and growing inside her.

Beatrice had visited Cordelia several times over the years, keeping track of her. She watched her grow from a wobbly toddler squealing as the surf touched her toes to the strong ocean swimmer she was by eight, to the young, quiet, curious girl she was today. Beatrice cherished this young girl who was so comfortable with her aloneness, so okay with just *being*. It was a rare trait in the humans, who seemed to always need to be doing something, making something, surrounded by people and things.

Cordelia...could just *be*. One of the reasons Cordelia's magic was so strong was because Cordelia was so good at simply being present—noticing everything around her. But now that she had begun to question and doubt herself—now was exactly when Cordelia needed Beatrice.

On this night, as the moonlight reflected on the water and light danced from wave to wave, Beatrice knew she'd find Cordelia on the Ananda Island pier as she had countless starry nights before.

Beatrice slowly began to swim towards Cordelia.

It was a particularly clear night and the light of the

stars from millions of years ago was breathtaking even to this old whale who had seen more night skies than she could ever keep track of. How anyone could look up at those stars and not believe in the magic, Beatrice would never understand.

Cordelia was lost in her thoughts as usual. *Oh my, this Child, she makes my heart ache with such joy.*

Even though Beatrice knew deep in her soul how special Cordelia was, she also knew nothing could prepare the girl for the moment when she realized she could hear a giant blue whale talk. Beatrice had no idea how Cordelia would react.

"Child. Child, can you hear me?" Beatrice whispered.

Cordelia sat straight up, goosebumps covering her flesh and making her shiver. *What is that? Is that a voice? Is it the wind?*

Cordelia was suddenly aware of a thickness in the air, like she'd been thrust inside an invisible cloud of static electricity. She heard a faint ringing in her ears.

"Cordelia, don't be scared, Child. Can you hear me?"

Cordelia wanted to run, but somehow seemed cemented to the spot. There was no doubt this time. She'd definitely heard a voice call her name. And it was coming from the blackness of the water. Never before had she felt unsafe at her beloved, favorite spot, but right now? She was scared.

"Who...who is that? Who's there," Cordelia stammered.

"Don't worry, I'm not here to harm you. I can't even get out of the water. I just want to talk to you," the voice answered from the darkness. Even though it sounded like it was part whisper, part ocean wave, the voice was clear, just like a human voice.

"Why can't you get out of the water? Is something wrong with your boat?"

"I'm not in a boat, I'm—"

"You're what?" Cordelia cut her off. "You better hurry up and make some sense because I live next door to Chief Edwards and I can run through these trees without any light and be there in five minutes."

"No need to call the police, Child. I hardly think they have a cell big enough to hold me in." Beatrice chuckled at the thought.

"Who are you? Where are you? Don't play games with me," Cordelia demanded.

"I'm not playing games, Cordelia." Beatrice paused and took a deep breath. "I'm a whale, a giant 904-year-old blue whale to be exact. My name is Beatrice and you...you can hear me."

6

The Beginning

"But..." Cordelia stammered as the words sank in, "how can I hear you...if you're a whale?"

"All humans can talk to most animals if they tried. But most humans are in such a hurry going from one place to another, worrying about this or that, that there's little chance of anyone being able to hear any more. Lots of humans used to hear the animals. But that was a long time ago."

Sure a trick was being played on her, Cordelia stood up. "Oh, really? Come closer so I can see you then...giant 904-year-old blue whale named Beatrice."

Cordelia was sure she was about to see a rowboat of her classmates pull up with a recording of some kind, and they would start laughing at her and call her a weirdo.

The water began to swish and sway up against the pilings, and suddenly Cordelia was looking into the giant eye of a massive whale catching the moonlight.

"Oh!"

Cordelia stumbled back, falling over her feet, landing hard on her bottom. She stared at the huge eye of the ancient blue whale. It stared back. And it was...beautiful.

"I... But...How...This can't be real...I don't understand... What...What's happening?"

"You're hearing my thoughts, Cordelia. You do hear me, don't you?"

"Yes," Cordelia whispered. "I hear you."

"That's real. I'm able to project my thoughts and make them into audible sound waves. You don't have to understand how I do this right now, but you can hear me. That proves what I've known for so many years. That I was right. You're the one."

Cordelia's mind was racing. Was she dreaming? Maybe this wasn't real. But if she *was* talking to a whale and a whale *was* talking back to her, she wanted answers.

"Why are you here?"

"I was drawn to you, Child. Drawn to you as if you were a beacon for my heart, finding my way home to you."

"Drawn to *me*? Why me?"

"I've been waiting for you for so long. Hoping to find someone like you for years...so many years...and finally, finally I felt you. The year you were born. I've been swimming by your island checking up on you, year after year, waiting until it was time to meet you. And why you? Because you're special, Cordelia."

A blue whale had been keeping track of her for her entire life? This was crazy. And amazing. And kind of...magical. She shook her head. "I'm nothing special, Beatrice. I'm just an ordinary girl—I don't even have any friends. People think I'm weird and strange. I'm not even ordinary."

"Oh, you are many things, so many things, and you're right—you are anything *but* ordinary. You're *extraordinary*, Cordelia. Of that, I'm certain."

Extraordinary?

"But...What if...What if I don't want to *be* extraordinary? What if I just want to be a regular, normal person?" *Extraordinary just seems like a special way of saying weird.*

Beatrice made a sound like a deep, heavy sigh. "You humans...all capable of so much. All able to do so very much...And yet...most humans do nothing with what they have. Humans see magic every day and call it luck or coincidence. So many are content to walk through their days half asleep, not realizing, not understanding."

"Understanding what?"

"Understanding that *everyone* is extraordinary. *Everyone is born* extraordinary. Born with so much magic. It stuns me how so few use it."

"*Magic*?"

"Oh yes, magic. Humans have abilities far greater than they realize. All of you! And every once in a while, a human—a very special human—is born into this world who can wake everyone else up. Born to shake sleepy human beings and jerk everyone out of their sleepwalking daze to make them understand the gifts so many are squandering. Someone like you to help humans remember that *everyone* is extraordinary."

"And you think...you think that's ...me?!"

"Child, I was not summoned to swim the vastness of the seven seas, searching for hundreds of years without a reason. I was sent, most definitely, for *you*. To teach *you*."

"Who sent you? And to teach me what exactly?"

Beatrice paused a moment. "Those are questions I can't answer yet, Cordelia. But eventually you'll have all the answers you need."

"But...I don't understand. This makes no sense. I'm talking to a whale! And you're talking back! It's just... *impossible*. And how are you 904 years old? How is *that* even possible?"

"I must go now, Child. I'm tired. It will all make sense in time. Meet me here again tomorrow night. I'll tell you more."

"Tomorrow night? But I can't come tomorrow, I have—" Cordelia stopped talking as the massive head gently slipped beneath the surface of the water. Cordelia stood staring at the slightly rippling water, hardly a trace that any of this had actually just happened.

What *had* just happened?

Cordelia walked home in a daze. You would've thought she would run home telling anyone who would listen she'd just spoken to a whale! *Out loud*. But the more she thought it over, even said it out loud to herself, "I just had a conversation with a whale. Yup, she talked to me and I talked back." Cordelia realized there was no way anyone would believe her. And besides, everyone thought she was weird enough already.

Mom and Dad were laughing at a TV show when she got home.

"Hey Cordelia, how was your day? You've been gone a while. Glad you found some things to do with your day. Janey says you never snuck in the back." Mom winked.

What? Janey told? She would have been irritated at her sister if she wasn't so distracted. "Yeah, I just walked around, talked with Ms. L. a little, then drew and read my book. I'm going to just go to my room to finish. I'm at a really good part."

Dad laughed at something on the TV. "Sounds good, Cord. There's leftover pizza on the counter if you're hungry. Janey went out with friends for dinner, so there's plenty." Her parents turned back to their show.

As usual, everything and everybody is normal...but me. Just when Ms. L. had made Cordelia feel like she was okay, a talking whale had shown up. And that? Was anything but normal. And definitely weird.

★ 44 ★

She couldn't sleep that night, staring at the gnarled, twisted limbs of the oak tree outside her bedroom window. *Am I crazy? Am I as weird as people think I am? Am I losing my mind and hearing voices?*

She thought about Beatrice calling her extraordinary. "I just want to feel okay, that's all. Can't I just be like everyone else? That would be so much easier." Cordelia whispered.

Just then Kalispell jumped onto the bed, climbed across Cordelia's stomach, and settled on her chest, staring into her eyes. Cordelia stared deep into the golden eyes of the cat she'd known for half her life.

"Kalispell, can you talk to me? Do *you* understand what I'm saying? If you can, *please* say something."

Kalispell continued to stare, then put her head down on her front paws, began to purr, and closed her eyes.

"Yeah. You're right. You should ignore me. That was weird. Even for me. Never mind."

As Cordelia finally drifted off to sleep thinking about how ridiculous the whole thing sounded—*A 904-year-old whale! Come ON!*—she decided she had somehow fallen asleep on the pier and dreamt up the whole fantastical thing.

7

Blueberry Pancakes and Blue Whales

Cordelia came into the kitchen the next morning smiling about her whale dream.

"What are you grinning about Cordi-pie?" Dad asked as he flipped a pancake.

"Daaaaad..." Her smile faded at the babyish nickname. Cordelia had outgrown it years ago, but Dad refused to acknowledge she was eleven, almost twelve in less than two weeks.

Dad held up his hands. "Sorry, sorry, old habits are hard to break. Why the big smile? And would you like one of my world famous blueberry pancakes? Mom and Janey are on morning duty at the store, so I thought I'd make breakfast for my Cordi—my *Cordelia*. Pancake?"

Dad was so goofy. Secretly, she still kind of liked the nickname, she just didn't want any kids at school to *ever* hear him say it. They didn't need any more ammunition.

"Just a really good dream. And yes, to pancakes. I'm starving!"

"You got in late last night. That's my girl! Worked up an appetite playing outside with some friends, did you? Did you remember to put on the bug repellent? You know how Mom is. If she sees you with a bunch of mosquito bites, she'll slather you in the stuff herself." He set a plate of pancakes in front of her.

"Uh, yeah, sure." Cordelia moved her bitten-up legs under the table. She stuffed a giant forkful of pancakes into her mouth. "Heh, Da, do blu whalls eber wim rund her?"

"How about you swallow first and ask me that again in English?" Dad sat down at the table with a cup of coffee.

Cordelia chewed faster, then swallowed. "Sorry. Do blue whales ever swim around here?"

"Blue whales have been found in every sea on the Earth. They don't generally come around here, though, but it's not completely unheard of. Why do you ask?"

"I had a dream about one last night. Her name was Beatrice. It made me curious." Cordelia forked another too-big bite of pancake into her mouth.

"Beatrice, hmm? Sounds like a whale of a dream, kid!" Cordelia groaned at the terrible Dad joke.

"We got in some new books yesterday at the store, I'm pretty sure we got one in about whales—actually, I know we did. Pretty cool coincidence. Come by later and take a look at it."

"Coincidence...Hunh."

"Yeah, you know when things happen—"

"Yes, I know what it means," Cordelia cut in. "The word just reminded me of something Beatrice said. In my dream."

Dad got up from the table. "Sounds like a pretty interesting dream, kiddo. You got clean up duty? I've got to get to the store. I think they should have all the new inventory unpacked by now." He winked.

"Sho, Da. I gwot it," Cordelia said, her mouth full.

"Cordelia, slow down, you'll choke! I made plenty of pancakes and you're the only one here. Stop talking with your mouth full!"

"Sorry. I'm just crazy hungry this morning! And they *are* the world's best pancakes, Dad."

"Okay, Cord. Run the dishwasher after you load it. See you later! Don't forget the sunscreen and bug spray. Love you!"

"Love you, too," she called as Dad left. Cordelia watched him walk down the path. She loved that her whole entire world was within walking distance.

Cordelia finished her breakfast, loaded and started the dishwasher, and got dressed. She couldn't wait to get her hands on that whale book.

8

McKenna's Seashell and Souvenir Shop

"**H**ey, Squirt! Guess you found something to do yesterday after all," Janey called down from up on a ladder just inside the door of the store.

"Yeah, I hung out at the pier all day." Cordelia looked around for Mom and Dad and not seeing either one of them, added, "But Dad thinks I was out with friends, so don't say anything, okay?"

Janey finished placing various touristy keepsakes—picture frames, seagull statues, sand castle snow globes—on the shelves and climbed down the ladder.

"Okay, but there's nothing wrong with being by yourself, you know. You don't have to lie to Mom and Dad."

"I know, but I just don't want them to worry," Cordelia sighed. "You don't understand. You have so many friends and everybody thinks you're cool."

Just then the bell on the front door jingled. Cordelia turned to look and the Greggs twins from her class walked in. The Greggs were from the wealthiest family on the island. The twins' dad was a CEO of some huge company and was almost never home. Their mother acted like she was some kind of "Queen of the Island," and nothing got approved or done on Ananda Island without the okay of Katie Greggs. People were afraid of her. And her daughters were just miniature versions of their mom. Whenever kids at school were making fun of Cordelia or calling her names, it seemed that the twins were always the ones starting it. They were mean and Cordelia didn't like them.

"Hi, Janey! Hi, Cordelia," both girls said in unison.

"Hi, Stella, hi, Margo," Janey said flatly. Janey knew they treated her sister the worst of all. "What can I help you with?"

"Our mother sent us. She has some guests coming and she wants some things for gift baskets. She said nothing too expensive and not too tacky. We thought your store was just the place!"

Cordelia felt her face get hot. "Why don't you two just—"

"We just got in some nice picture frames and wine glasses," Janey said quickly, cutting Cordelia off.

The twins looked from Cordelia to Janey, their heads turning identically. "Sounds perfect," said Margo.

"Mother will love that. Show us," demanded Stella.

"They're right over there. You can find them on your own," Cordelia said, her heart pounding.

"Oh! She talks!? Nice customer service," said Margo. "But then, what do you expect from someone who just sits there looking weird all day long and who only talks to a goldfish."

"Okay, enough." Janey grabbed the twins by their elbows and ushered them over to the wine glass display.

"Ow! You're hurting us!"

"No I'm not. Now pick out what you want. I'll be happy to gift wrap anything for you," Janey said loudly. Then in a hushed, angry whisper she added, "If I ever hear you call my sister weird again, I'll do way more than squeeze your elbows. And I don't care who your parents are. Understand me?"

Stella and Margo looked scared. Janey was a good foot taller than them, not to mention strong and muscular from her many years playing various sports.

"Say you understand me," Janey demanded.

"Yes...we do," Margo said quietly.

"Sure." Stella said more defiantly. "Come on, Margo. I think everything here is *way* too tacky. We need to shop somewhere else. Let's go."

The twins left and Janey walked back over to Cordelia. She wrapped an arm around her shoulder and said in a low voice, "Ignore those two snobs. Being cool is over-rated. I'd rather be smart and weird like you any day. I love you, Squirt."

Cordelia fought back tears. "Thanks, Janey." She hugged her sister.

"So, what are you here for anyway?"

Beatrice popped back into Cordelia's head and the cloud over her lifted. "A whale book! Dad said a new one came in. Do you know where it is?"

"Oh, yeah! It looks great. It's in the back on the top shelf. I'll come help you get it."

Just then the front door jingled again. A huge family of vacationers in sunglasses, hats, and sunscreen all over their noses walked in looking ready to spend money.

"I got it, no worries," Cordelia waved Janey off. "Help the customers; I have a magical childhood to go have."

Janey snort-laughed. "Later, Squirt!"

9

The Bookshelf

Cordelia walked to the back of the store where her parents had created a small book nook. The nook's walls made a 'U' shape and were filled with shelves of books. At the back of the "U" were two comfy, soft leather chairs, a small table, and a lamp. In the off season, Cordelia went there straight after school, did her homework, then read for hours. Cordelia loved going there almost as much as she loved going to the pier, but during the summers Mom said she had to leave the chairs free for customers.

Dad displayed brand new titles on the upper shelves. Cordelia spotted the whale book. The large gift book was on the highest shelf. Cordelia tried to reach it, but was too short, her fingertips didn't even brush the edge of the shelf. *Ugh! When am I gonna grow already?*

She'd have to go find a stepstool or get Janey to reach it for her after all. She decided to try one more time. Cordelia got up on her tiptoes and strained to make her body as tall as she could, willing herself to reach the book.

Just then a strange crackling sound filled Cordelia's head and tiny shocks of static electricity shot through her body up through her fingertips. The next thing she knew, Cordelia was a little light-headed and she was holding the whale book in her hands.

Huh. That's weird. She looked up at the high shelf and back down at the book. The blue whale on the cover got her so excited she shrugged off the strange staticky feeling and sat in one of the big, comfy chairs.

Cordelia immediately got lost in the pages of the book about the giant sea creatures.

"Hey, kiddo! You found it!" Dad snapped on the small lamp next to Cordelia. "It's dark back here; don't read without the light. Bad for your eyes."

"Hunh?"

Cordelia looked up, startled, and blinked her eyes to refocus. She had no idea how long she'd been there.

"Good book? You hungry? Want a sandwich from

the cafe? It's way past lunchtime. Even after all those pancakes you must be hungry by now."

"Dad! Did you know that a blue whale's tongue weighs as much as an elephant? Its heart is as big as half of a car. Did you know it isn't just the biggest mammal in the ocean, it's the biggest mammal in the history of the planet! A baby whale is called a calf. If there's a large group of whales, it's called a pod. And you're right, they migrate all over the world – all seven seas! But in the water around Sri Lanka, there are blue whales that stay all year round! There's this lady scientist there studying why—"

"Whoa there, Cordi! Slow down. I guess you've been here a while. Did you read that whole book?"

"Not even close! There's so much information. I need to read it all! Dad," Cordelia got a serious tone, "I need this book. Need."

"Cordi, it's a fifty dollar book. I can't just give it to you, you know that."

"I'll buy it. I still have birthday money left from last year! Can I take it with me and go get my money? I'll bring the money right back. Just don't let anyone buy it while I'm gone." Cordelia's words were coming out so fast Dad was starting to laugh.

"Wow. That must have been some dream you had last night. And that must be some book. I'll order another to replace this one. You can give me the money tonight. I trust you. I know where you live, remember?"

"Thanks, Dad. I want to finish this whole book tonight. It's amazing!"

"You know I can't say no to you, Cord. Enjoy the book. You can stay here and read, it's kind of slow today—it's so gorgeous that all the tourists are at the beach. But don't forget about the softball game tonight. We're up against the Greggs' team. I need you cheering me on!"

Cordelia remembered the part of the dream where Beatrice had said to come back the next night—tonight. *What if...what if it wasn't a dream? It had to be, right?* But thinking about the dream, it sure seemed so...real. Cordelia looked at the whale book.

"You know what?" Dad said gently. "Forget it. Janey's coming and playing first base. You go read about your blue whale. Bertha was it?"

"Beatrice, Dad. And thanks—I'll come to the next game—promise!"

"Anytime." Dad looked around, then added, "Cordi-Pie!" He laughed. "Love you, come have lunch with me soon!"

"Will do!" But Cordelia never did. She didn't stop reading until the store closed. Mom, Dad, and Janey headed off to the softball field and Cordelia said she was going home to read. But when she got back to the house, she packed her tote bag and headed to the pier. She had a whale to meet. Or at least she thought she might.

10

Questions

Cordelia arrived at the pier just as the sun was setting. She took in a deep breath and stood still. She never got tired of this view. It always made her feel...safe. Her family was not religious, but Cordelia imagined that church must feel a lot like being out on the pier. It seemed to her, that people went to church to make them feel better about the world, to help make sense of others and themselves. That's what being near the ocean did for Cordelia.

There were so many questions Cordelia had about why the world was the way it was. Why do people act the way they do? Why are some people so mean? Why is being alone sometimes so much easier than being with others? Cordelia thought about Ms. L. saying there was no such thing as normal. Was that really true, or was her kind elderly neighbor just trying to make her feel better? And Beatrice...she had called her *extraordinary*. How could *that* possibly be true? So many questions. She wasn't sure if any religion could answer any of these question any better than the ocean and the stars could.

Out here, especially at night, the answers she longed to know were right in front of her. She just...*knew* it. The ocean waves, the stars, the breeze—all of them seemed to be whispering the answers. Cordelia knew she was somehow connected to those whispers, she was a part of them, and she swore, the more she visited here, the more she could hear what they were saying. And if Beatrice was real, she was going to ask those whale whispers for answers.

Cordelia was thinking about all the facts she had learned about blue whales. They swam in pods, but, more often they would travel the globe alone. Cordelia loved that. She had something in common with the largest animal in the history of the world.

Maybe if a blue whale is okay traveling the deepest waters of the seas all alone—and being just fine with it—maybe I'm really fine, too, just like Ms. L. said. Me and a giant blue whale. We have something in common. How cool is that?

Even though Cordelia was sure Beatrice was just a dream—and it was an outlandish, illogical thought— what if the talking blue whale *did* show up again tonight?

Cordelia decided she would ask that whale if she liked to be alone, too, preferred it even, just like she did.

11

Not A Dream

As usual, Cordelia had gotten lost in her thoughts and lost track of time. She'd been lying on the pier, watching the stars come out.

She knew all the names and stories of the constellations by heart—last summer's obsession. She followed Draco the Dragon's tale, knowing it would lead her to the handle of the Big Dipper—Ursa Major—which would lead her to the Little Dipper—Ursa Minor. "Ursa" meant "bear." She was imagining that mother and baby bear when the water started to shift and splash the pilings.

Cordelia bolted upright and peered out at the water. "Hello," she said, both scared and excited.

"Hello," a slow, soothing voice replied. "I'm so glad you came back, Child."

"Beatrice!"

Cordelia's heart raced. She felt no fear now, only excitement. *It wasn't a dream!* But Cordelia couldn't see the whale. She only heard her. "You're real! I hoped, but I didn't really believe it. It just couldn't be... Where are you? How can I hear you, but not see you? Please let me see you, please?" All her words tumbled together.

Suddenly, cascades of water began falling as a large mass broke through the water. And Cordelia found herself staring into the gigantic eye of the blue whale.

"How are you doing this, Beatrice? How can I hear you talking to me?"

"I know it seems strange to you, but I can connect with your thoughts, get inside your brain. I can send information to you because I'm able to connect to you through your energy. Right now, you can hear me with your ears because I'm transferring my thoughts into an audible frequency for you. But eventually, I'll teach you how to talk to me with just your mind."

"You can read my mind? Like telepathy?" Cordelia panicked a little at the idea of anyone, even a talking whale, being able to know what she was thinking.

"Telepathy is a simple way of describing it, but it's more than that, Cordelia. And no, I cannot read your

mind or know what you're thinking, unless you let me. We'd have to connect on the same energy wave and you'd have to allow me the access. A better term for what I'm doing is 'energy connecting.' It's when two energies connect on the deepest level, allowing each other access, so they overlap and communicate directly. It's a very efficient tool."

"Um, what?"

"I know it sounds complicated, but it's actually not." Beatrice paused. "Do you know how light works, Cordelia?"

"Yes! I studied it a few months ago in science class. Light is made of energy that travels in waves like the water in the ocean. It can look like different colors to us depending on how long the waves are, and we can only see some light depending on how fast the light wave is moving."

"That's right," said Beatrice.

Cordelia pointed to the sky. "The light from those stars, it's been traveling millions and millions, maybe billions of years, just to get to this spot, right now, for us to see it. Isn't that amazing? Knowing that little tiny light wave traveled all this way, and now we get to see it? It's... magical, Beatrice, that's what it is."

"You're just as they said you would be, Child. Curious, full of energy, and so intelligent. I see now why it was you I was searching for."

For the first time in her life, Cordelia felt like she was exactly who she was supposed to be, exactly as she was. Maybe she wasn't weird or different, maybe she belonged to this world...maybe she fit here perfectly—like a puzzle piece that had just been placed in exactly the right spot. Finally.

"Tell me more, Beatrice."

"Keep thinking of those light waves. You can hear what I'm saying because I'm connecting with you through energy waves like the light. It's very complex, yet elegantly simple. All living creatures emit their own unique energy waves, and we can connect together through them. Right now, my energy waves and your energy waves are connecting and communicating in the spots where our energies overlap. When we connect at the deepest level—when we don't just communicate but allow ourselves to *feel* each other's energy—we actually become part of each other."

"So, together we create our own energy wave and in that spot we can communicate?"

"Yes, yes, just like that. Exactly! We're creating our own unique energy wave—a perfect way to phrase it!"

"So," Cordelia said, "I can connect with you if I can find your...your energy wave? I can talk to you by just thinking, not actually saying words out loud?"

"Eventually you'll be able to connect with me more deeply like that, but it does take time, and lots of energy. I've had hundreds of years of practice, and I still get very tired after I energy connect. It used to be much easier for me. I hardly had to rest very much after, but, I was a much younger whale back then."

"A younger whale? When did you—"

"As I said, I've been searching for you for a long time, Child. I've met many souls during that time."

"Wow..." Cordelia thought about all the others Beatrice talked to on her journey. "I want to try!"

Cordelia closed her eyes and concentrated on Beatrice. She willed her thoughts to the whale, imagining their energy waves connecting and overlapping. She kept at it for a good minute and then let out a huge gasp, not realizing she'd been holding her breath. "Anything?"

"No, sweet girl. But I do love your enthusiasm to jump right in and try! It will take time. Have patience. You'll get there soon enough. You have far more extraordinary gifts than energy connecting to discover."

"Gifts? I have gifts? I love the idea of all of this, but my brain is still telling me none of this is real and I must be stuck in a dream—an amazing dream I don't ever want to wake up from—but still, a dream. It's all just..."

"It's bizarre and confusing to you. I come from a time when the earth was supposed to evolve in a very different way. But things changed. I'm left over from a realm you humans would deem magical, I suppose."

"So...magic is real?"

"Yes...I'll try to explain. There's knowledge in the minds of all humans—knowledge as vast as the universe inside each of you. It's information that's existed forever. They're things that cannot be learned, only discovered—because they just...simply...*are*.

Part of this knowledge is a magical universal energy. It's a force field running through this mighty universe—holding all of us together. We are all intertwined—the stars, the planets, the animals, the people. We're all as connected and necessary to each other as your heart is to your lungs—as necessary as your breathing is to your very life. This energy force is a part of us, running through all of us."

"Kind of like gravity," asked Cordelia.

"Sort of. But bigger. It's so much...*more*. It's a force that entangles us together, allowing each of us to communicate with each other. It's a magical, ever-present force that makes you belong to me and me belong to you. We all belong to each other. We are, all of us, indivisible. And I am here to teach you not only how to summon this magical force, but also how to use it and connect with it."

"Magical force? Like Star Wars? That's pretend, Beatrice. From a movie. And magic isn't real, it's just tricks." Cordelia shook her head.

"Chiiiiild." Beatrice drew out the word very whale-like in one long syllable. "Like I said, we're all born with the knowledge of the universe. We all *have* access to it, just most humans don't know *how* to access it. But, nonetheless, the knowledge is there, the force is real, and the magic? It's very real. And once you learn, you'll see it's everywhere you look."

Beatrice had just confirmed what Cordelia had always thought, and hoped was true. "It is, isn't it, Beatrice? The answers are all around us, right in front of us? Like, the magic?"

"Oh yes, and the truth and magic of this world are as plain as the nose on your face once you know how to see it."

"I knew it. Because I *felt* it somehow—and heard it, like whispers on the ocean waves. What can I do once you teach me to 'summon this magical force,' Beatrice? What then?"

"Dear sweet Child, anything. You'll be able do just about anything. You're extraordinarily gifted, that's quite clear."

"So, I'll be able to talk with animals with just my thoughts?"

★ 76 ★

"That's just the start, Cordelia. Think bigger, so much bigger. You'll be able to connect with every being and everything. But there's more." Beatrice paused.

"What? What else will I be able to do? What else?"

"Oh, Child, you...you shall be able to fly!"

"Wait. Fly? Like in the sky? Actually...*fly*?"

"It's no metaphor. We begin tomorrow. Go home and get some rest. You'll need it. I told you, this work will take a lot of your energy."

"Beatrice, if I can't even find your energy waves, how am I supposed to be able to *fly*?"

"Connecting with others is far harder than connecting with yourself. You'll understand in time."

"I just don't want to disappoint you. I know you think I'm special, but I'm happy just feeling like I belong for the first time in my life." Then Cordelia faltered. "But what if I'm not as magical as you think? What if I'm not good enough, Beatrice?"

"First of all, the fact that we're having this conversation at all means you're already so much more than enough. Listen to me. So many people accept so much less, Cordelia. So many people are okay with good enough and close enough when they can be so much *more*. If people would just realize they can be extraordinary, their lives would change drastically."

"Why don't they then?"

"Because what people fear more than failure, even more than they fear success, is *change*, Cordelia. Once you realize that you're capable of being extraordinary, you no longer have an excuse to be less than that. To know how truly capable you are is to have to change your own expectations of yourself. And that? Seems to be more than most people can handle."

"Beatrice?"

"Yes, Child?"

"I don't want to be just normal. I want to know what I can do, who I can be. I need to know. I want to be... extraordinary. Please teach me."

Beatrice's great body swelled and shifted at Cordelia's words, sending water lapping up onto the pier. "I knew you would not let me down, my magical, extraordinary Cordelia. We begin tomorrow."

"Good night, Beatrice...and...thank you. Thank you for looking for me for all those years—and finding me." Cordelia looked up at the night sky, sending her thanks to the stars, the moon, and the entirety of the magnificent, magical universe.

"It is my honor and my privilege, Child. Good night."

"Wait, one last question," Cordelia said before Beatrice disappeared.

"Yes?"

"You swim alone, right? You've traveled all these years...alone?"

"Yes, for the most part. Sometimes I cross paths with a particularly interesting blue whale or another sea creature and we swim along for miles, sharing our adventures. But I do usually travel alone. I enjoy just thinking my thoughts most of the time. I prefer being alone, I suppose. Why do you ask?"

Cordelia's smile stretched across her face. "Just wondering. No real reason. I'm like that, too."

"I know, Child, I know."

Beatrice slipped under the waves.

Cordelia walked home smiling, the feeling of belonging and connection getting stronger with every step.

But...fly? How?

12

The Day

Cordelia woke up later than normal. She was starving. Connecting with Beatrice must use lots of energy, and she figured that's why she'd been so hungry the past two mornings.

In the kitchen she saw a note on the fridge.

Cordi,

Didn't want to wake you.

Dad got donuts.

Fruit in the fridge.

Stop by the store for lunch.

Have a great day! Love you!

Mom

Yum! Donut Palace donuts! Dad must have won the game last night. Her father only got donuts if he woke up in a great mood or it was a special occasion. Seemed like both things were true.

She set one glazed and one chocolate sprinkled on a plate. She was happily munching and licking her fingers when she heard something.

"Cordelia? Can you hear me, Child?" Beatrice's voice filled up the kitchen.

Okay, this is just crazy! Beatrice can talk to me even when we're not together? In my house?

"Yes..." Cordelia looked around, grateful no one was home. "I can hear you."

Kalispell meowed. "Can you hear her, too, Kalispell?"

As Beatrice spoke, Kalispell started to purr.

"Oh good. You can hear me. Come to the pier this morning. There isn't much boating traffic and it will be easier to begin teaching you in the daylight."

"Um, are you sure? What if someone sees you? A blue whale will attract a lot of attention. Not to mention a talking one."

"I'll be able to sense anyone coming. I can dive low if I

need. Come as soon as you're done eating. And don't let that cat get your donut; she's just about to grab it."

Kalispell had leapt onto the table and was about to take a bite of her donut. Cordelia shooed her away. "But... how did you know that? How can you see?"

But there was no response. Beatrice seemed to have disconnected, like hanging up the phone.

Cordelia gobbled down her donuts in stunned silence, then raced to get dressed and pack up her tote bag. She grabbed some bananas, some string cheese, a granola bar, and one more donut to eat on the way.

"See ya later, Kalispell. You and Charles should energy connect! Maybe he can catch some fish for you!" Cordelia laughed and left the house.

13

The Leaf

Before Cordelia got to the pier or could even see Beatrice, she heard her. "Grab a handful of leaves before you get out here, please."

Cordelia grabbed some palm fronds from the ground. She put them in her tote and walked quickly to the end of the pier.

Beatrice was right, she didn't see any boats at all. She looked up into the clear blue sky—no planes either.

Just then, Beatrice surfaced. "I'm glad I could connect with you at your house. That's good. The magic is so strong with you. I'm going to keep talking to you, but from below the water. There's less risk of me being spotted that way. It's going to be easier for you to learn in the daylight, so I'll be swimming below as much as I can while I instruct you, okay?"

"Okay. The day *is* better—another late night and my parents would start asking questions. But stay below. A blue whale sighting on the island? It would be huge news."

"Agreed. Better to go unnoticed. I'm going under."

"Hey! I read blue whales can hold their breath for a long time. Is that true?" Cordelia asked.

"I can hold my breath up to twenty minutes if I need to—so I won't need to surface too much while I'm teaching you. This first lesson won't take that long."

Amazing...just...amazing. Beatrice swam away from the pier, then began her dive. Her huge head and back broke the surface of the water, and Cordelia could see the elegant curve of her spine. As Beatrice dove, the rest of her body followed, her spine a seemingly endless line disappearing into the water. Beatrice was huge! Finally, her massive fluke broke the surface, creating a giant waterfall in the ocean. The water streamed from her tail's edges, until it too followed the rest of her deep under the ocean.

"You are the most beautiful creature I've ever seen," Cordelia exclaimed.

"Thank you, Child; I agree. Which is why I chose to be a blue whale so many years ago."

"Chose? What do you mean you chose to be a blue whale?"

"Another lesson for another time. Now, let's begin; you'll need all your energy. Get out a leaf and put it on the pier."

Cordelia placed a palm frond on the pier. "Okay, done."

"Now, concentrate on that leaf. Imagine it's nothing more than atoms, little balls of energy held together with the same energy force that holds together you and me. You're not so different from the leaf, Cordelia. You're the same—you're both just energy. Imagine seeing those energy waves, both yours and the leaf's. Feel the energy of both your waves. Imagine them overlapping, and feel how it's stronger where you both connect in those overlapping spots. In your mind, stay in that spot. Feel it, stay there—then, think about the leaf rising into the air. Use the energy you feel to make the leaf float up off the pier."

"Beatrice, you're kidding right? You think I can make this leaf float up off the pier? I can't."

"First of all, never say you can't. Your thoughts and words have power and energy, Cordelia. The words you say fly out into the universe and gather power, and are connected to you forever. Whether they are negative or positive, they *will* stay connected to you. You *can* and you *will*. Say it, but most importantly, *believe it*." Beatrice's voice sounded almost stern.

"Okay, here goes," Cordelia shrugged. "I can do this. I will do this." Cordelia imagined seeing the atoms of the leaf all swirling and glowing with the energy holding it together. She imagined seeing the leaf's energy waves flowing off in all directions. She imagined seeing her own energy waves coming off her fingertips, hovering over the leaf. Finally, she imagined their two energy waves swirling together, connecting up, intersecting, growing and pulsing larger and larger where they overlapped. She could imagine it all so clearly that she could almost see it, and she swore she could feel it, too. It all began to make sense in her mind.

But nothing happened. The leaf didn't fly. She took a break, walked around, and tried again. For over an hour, with Beatrice's encouragement, Cordelia tried again and again until she was exhausted.

"Ugh! If I can't make a leaf fly, how can I ever fly myself," groaned Cordelia.

"Because once you know, you'll know. It's just a shift in your mind—a slight shift from what is to what can be.

It's choosing the positive versus the negative. Embrace the possibility of what can be, Cordelia. In doing that, you will find your magic. Believe, Cordelia. You must believe with all your might. Let go of doubts. Let go of wondering *how*. You already know how. Your job, your only job, is to believe with all your heart and soul that you *can*."

And with that, there was a shift in Cordelia. A simple, tiny shift in her thinking that unlocked something inside her brain. She couldn't explain it out loud—but she knew it had existed all along. She was tapping into that bank of universal knowledge. A hum of electricity began to buzz from deep inside her. The hairs on her arms stood up. She understood and she believed.

Cordelia looked up at the clouds and the pelicans flying by. She looked over to the tall pine trees.

Then Cordelia closed her eyes.

She rose up into the air.

She was near the shoreline and almost as high as the tree line on the shore when Beatrice called out. "Child!! Child, get down here this instant! It's broad daylight! You can't just go flying about! Someone will see you! And I can tell you this—they are not ready. Come down now!"

Cordelia's eyes popped open. "Down! Now!" Beatrice's head was just beneath the water.

Cordelia wanted to obey, but she hesitated. She marveled at the world as she had never seen it before. Cordelia didn't want to come down. She wanted to soar across the water, race with the dolphins, and fly with the pelicans—like in her dream with Charles! She wanted to stay up here forever.

Suddenly though, Cordelia was tired—very tired. If she didn't go back down right away, she knew she would fall.

So Cordelia forced herself to float back to the ground, surprising herself with how much control she had.

"Sorry, Beatrice. I wasn't ignoring you. It was just so... so wonderful."

"I know, sweet Child, oh how I know."

"I didn't want to come down, but I felt...I felt like I was running out of gas. Like a car on empty. I think I would have fallen."

"Yes, you would have. I'm glad you trusted your instincts. I need to teach you how to summon the universal energy at will, and also how to keep it. You just jumped a few lessons ahead." Cordelia thought she heard pride in Beatrice's voice.

"Now! Teach me now, Beatrice. Oh, please!"

"You haven't the energy right now, Cordelia. You need to rest. You'll be very tired for a while, I suspect. Go home. Go rest. You did so well, Child, so well. I, too, must rest. I get very tired these days."

"Okay, but I'll be back soon," Cordelia said, pride in her own voice.

Cordelia walked home filled with a boundless energy, paired with a tiredness she had never before experienced in her life.

When Mom got home, she found Cordelia tucked up in bed, sound asleep.

14

All the Wonders

Cordelia woke up late again the next day. The kitchen clock read 1:45 p.m. *Whoa, I slept over twenty-four hours! Good thing no one is here to wonder about that. I guess Beatrice was right.*

Cordelia made herself two peanut butter and banana sandwiches and poured herself a large glass of milk.

As she mindlessly ate the sandwiches, she thought about the amazing feeling of bobbing in the air. She needed to do that again. *I can't wait to fly some more, Beatrice! I'll be there soon!*

Just as she thought those words, a shiver ran through Cordelia's body. And then she realized she'd not only felt that yesterday, but also when she'd reached for the book about whales at the store. "Yes! I must have floated to that book!" That she'd had these powers even before she'd met Beatrice was just occurring to her when she heard Beatrice's voice inside her head.

"Don't come to the pier until nightfall, Child. There are too many boats out today, too many people. Come tonight as the sun is setting. It will be safer."

Cordelia stopped chewing. Her mouth was full of peanut butter and banana. *What was happening?*

"Yes, Child, it's me. I heard you call out to me with your mind. You've begun to energy connect at the deepest level. You no longer have to speak your words to me—we can connect using only our thoughts now. Your magic is so strong. I knew once it began it would be quick, but even I'm surprised by how swiftly you're learning and adapting."

"You mean...you can *hear* my thoughts now?"

"Yes. You don't have to speak out loud to me anymore. Try it by just thinking to me again."

"Oh, I don't know if I can do that."

"You just did. Try again."

"Okay. I'll try. Let me know if this works."

"Hey, Squirt. Who you talking to?" Janey appeared from around the corner.

Cordelia whirled around. "What?!"

"You were talking to someone. I heard you. You were so into it you didn't even hear me say hello. Who were you talking to?"

"Why are you home?" Cordelia asked, trying to change the subject.

"Because you came home yesterday before lunch and went right to bed. Mom was worried you might be getting a cold, so she had me stay home today. You slept all day. And now you're talking to yourself. You feeling okay, Cordi?"

Cordelia had to think fast.

"I brought food out to the pier yesterday. I wasn't hungry when I got home. I was feeling a little tired I guess, probably just too much sun. I've been...thinking about a story I'm writing. I...want to draw the pictures, too. I guess I didn't realize I was talking out loud."

Janey squinted at Cordelia. "Nothing else is up? Those twins aren't bothering you again, are they?"

"Nope, just weird Cordelia being weird. Promise." It looked like Janey was buying her story.

"Fine. And don't call yourself weird. You're just like everyone else. We're all kinda weird, some of us just hide it a little better than others. Now, gimme a bite of that, I'm starving!" Janey grabbed one of Cordelia's sandwiches.

"Janey, I'm not like everyone else. I know that. And it's okay. I like who I am. Really."

"You're amazing, you know that, Squirt? You are."

And for the first time ever, Cordelia truly believed those words.

"Try now," Beatrice's voice whispered in her head.

And that was the first time, while she was eating peanut butter and banana sandwiches with her sister, Cordelia discovered she could talk with a giant blue whale, using only her mind.

15

Connecting

After Janey was sure Cordelia was okay, she went out with some friends. Cordelia spent the rest of her afternoon on her bed, waiting for evening to come, drawing in her sketchbook and talking with Beatrice—all without saying a word out loud.

Cordelia learned she had to imagine Beatrice as if she was right in front of her in order to connect with her. The more details she could imagine, like smells and sounds, the easier it was to connect. Salty sea air, lapping waves, and squawking seagulls filled her senses and focused her mind. She had to think most about the energy waves Beatrice emitted. If she visualized those waves as light coming off her friend, it was easiest. She imagined energy glowing like sun beams shooting out from Beatrice. Then she imagined her own energy glowing and spreading until their two energy waves finally overlapped. When their energies connected, their thoughts could connect, too.

"It seems so easy, like I've always known how to do this, Beatrice."

"You have. As I told you before, the entire knowledge of the universe is at your fingertips. You just have to learn how to access it."

"Can I do this with others...? Like with Janey?"

"Once you teach her, yes. And others, too."

Cordelia could hardly bear to think about Janey going away to college. So many changes would happen when Janey left. But if she could connect with her..."Beatrice! Janey can still be with me! Even when she's away!"

"Exactly. The more you learn, the more you'll realize we're never really ever alone. We're all so completely connected to each other that distance and time have no meaning—at least not like how humans think of them. No one ever has to be truly alone if they don't want to be—because in reality it's an impossibility to be alone." Beatrice paused. "The concept of 'alone' doesn't even make sense."

"I don't mind being alone. I like it."

"I do, too, but that's not what I mean. Even if you *choose* to be physically by yourself, you can't actually *be* alone. We all exist *because* of each other—each of us are puzzle pieces that all fit together. So even in your most alone moments, you're still connected to the entirety of the universe. It's almost an absurd notion to consider *alone* as a possible state of being. It simply *cannot be.* The universe is utterly dependent on you being a part of it."

"Whoa. When you put it that way, I guess I really do matter, huh?" Cordelia suddenly felt proud of being a part of something so incredible.

"Everyone matters. And the part you play is so much bigger, so much...*more* than you can imagine. While I have existed for 904 years, I continue to be astonished at what I continue to learn."

"Oh, yes! I wanted to ask you about that. How are you 904 years old? This book says you have about the same life span as a human."

"That, Child, is a long story."

"Tell me. Please?"

"I suppose we do have time to pass before nightfall. Where to begin? First, I need you to keep an open mind.

It involves science not yet discovered on Earth. You'll have to accept the unknown. Can you do that?"

"Beatrice, I think we're past that, don't you? In the last few days, I've spoken with a whale, flown in the air, and now I'm using my mind to talk to you! I have no idea how any of that works, but I'm doing it all. I promise to be okay with not understanding how it's all possible."

"Excellent points, my dear, excellent points. To begin, much of what scientists on Earth have discovered is true. Their progress has been remarkable. But there's so much humans don't understand, and it's simply because humans are limited in their perspective. It's like an ant on a mountain top. It cannot actually know of the mountain's scope, its height. An ant can be on a leaf, but it cannot know the tree itself as a whole. It can't know of the stars, the moon, of human existence. It can't know because it can only experience life from its own ant perspective, which is terribly limiting." Beatrice paused. "With me so far?"

"Yes, makes sense." Cordelia had subconsciously started sketching ants walking along leaves.

"Now, take humans. You know of the stars, the moon, the laws that seem to govern your planet. You know what you can physically experience. You can wonder and imagine, but you simply cannot know what else exists because you're limited by being human. There are so many more dimensions and so many more universes out there. All you can know are the ones you experience, so, like the ant, it seems this is all there is. But, there are other worlds that exist, worlds beyond the scope of human comprehension. Humans are just as limited as ants. Understand?"

"Yes, I think so."

Beatrice continued. "My body, this physical whale body, is only about ninety years old. But my energy body, what humans call the soul, is a lot older. You're correct when you say a whale's lifespan is about the same as a human's, and this is where it gets complicated. My physical body is ninety years old, but I've been using it for more than 250 years, and my soul is 904 years old."

"Okay, yeah, um, I'm trying but whoa...what?"

"Here's where you must open your mind to possibilities, Child. There are several vortexes on your Earth. A vortex is a tunnel in the universal energy field that connects with other dimensions, other universes. If one knows where a vortex is and how to enter it, you can cross over between worlds. When I first came through from my world to yours, I chose to enter as a whale. I retained all the knowledge of my soul's past experiences. I know how to access the vortex and go back and forth. Still with me?"

"Let me see. So our souls are actually energy. And that energy is who we *really* are—not our physical bodies. And our souls can pass, if we know how, through vortexes on the Earth to other dimensions and other universes?"

"Yes, that's it exactly," Beatrice said.

"But, what do you mean you chose to be a whale?"

"Some souls, like me, can come through vortexes on your planet and choose what form they want to experience their lives in. What better choice than the breathtaking blue whale? Would you not choose something so magnificent?"

"Yes...yes I think I would—or at least I hope I would. It sounds...amazing. These vortexes, where are they?"

"All over the Earth. On land, the air, the sea."

"Where is *your* vortex, the one you use?"

"Mine? Off the coast of Sri Lanka there's an excellent vortex. Scientists are getting very curious about the spot. A good many blue whales stay there year round. Scientists can't figure out why. They think it's the food supply, but that's far from the only reason."

"Oh! I read about Sri Lanka! So are there other blue whales there, whales like you? Like really old ones?"

"Yes, many. Many souls choose to come back as animals, particularly blue whales. We're drawn to the grace and beauty of the blue whale. To inhabit the body of the largest animal this Earth has ever known is quite something to experience when you realize you can."

"But wouldn't you rather be in a human body? Doesn't being a whale make things harder to do?"

"Oh Child, to be a human is the most limiting creature of all. Humans get so caught up in opinions, emotions, power, and greed. Not to mention, human bodies wear out so quickly. Most animals contain souls that are far more evolved than humans are. Many souls come back as animals to experience unconditional love and joy."

"So...So, is every soul that comes here on some kind of a mission like you? To find someone like me?"

"No. I was the only one asked to take on this mission. Most souls, if they choose to come back to this universe, on this planet, are coming back to grow their soul energy—to learn and to evolve. But most humans on Earth are first soul humans."

"First soul?"

"That means this is the first lifetime of your soul here on Earth. Your soul was created and put into a human form in this universal dimension. Right now your soul energy and your physical body are the same age."

"But you said you've been using your body for 250 years. How is that possible?"

"Because I arrived from another dimension to your world through a vortex. I can go back and forth through the vortex as I please. When I leave this dimension, my body stays in the vortex, not aging until I return. Time, as you know it, does not exist in the vortex—it's just a holding spot. While my soul travels between dimensions, my physical body on Earth does not age."

"I get it! Your soul has existed for a total of 904 years from your beginning until now, with trips through vortexes with many different bodies? Cool!"

"Yes! Exactly! It is, as you say, cool."

Beatrice's laugh sounded like surf pounding the beach.

"Did you come back and forth through the vortex often while you were looking for me?"

"Yes. I would go back to my home dimension to continue my learning in between searching for you."

"Your learning?"

"Oh yes, the knowledge of the universe exists for all of us to discover, but like everything, it takes time. Patience is a valuable skill when one begins to understand universal eternity and collective consciousness."

"Universal eternity? Collective consciousness? What?" Cordelia's head was spinning.

"Child, I'm getting tired. I fear I cannot briefly explain those concepts. We can talk more about those things another day. You truly are an endlessly curious soul."

"But one last thing before you rest, okay? Can... can I, will I...be able to travel like you soon? To other dimensions? Through vortexes? Will you teach me?"

"No, sweet girl. While you were born with more magic and knowledge than a human has been born with in hundreds and hundreds of years, traveling to other worlds is something you cannot do right now."

"But why not?"

"Because this is the first energy cycle of your soul. You're a first soul human. You can only pass back and forth after your soul energy has passed through to the next dimension naturally. After that, you may decide where to go next, but not before."

"You mean after I die? I go to another dimension? Like heaven?"

"Sort of. Many humans call it heaven because that's as close to an explanation as they can come up with. Religions try so hard to explain it, and they get close, but humans cannot know what they cannot know. Think of the ant again. While the physical body wears out, the soul never dies. Energy—and the soul is nothing but energy— can never be destroyed. It just changes form."

"Yes! We learned all about energy changing forms in science this year!"

"Good. Once you pass through the vortex for the first time, you'll understand that you're part of something immense, magical. You'll understand that who you are is exactly who you needed to be here on Earth. Most importantly, you will truly be able to conceive of how very much you matter."

Cordelia's eyes welled with tears. "Oh, Beatrice. I think that's the best, most wonderful thing I've ever heard," Cordelia whispered, this time not just in her thoughts, but out loud.

"It's even more wonderful than I can ever describe in words, Child. Believe that. I must go rest now. We have a big night ahead of us. Nap if you can."

The whale's last four words drifted off like a whisper in the wind as Beatrice faded from Cordelia's mind.

Cordelia did not realize she'd been drawing the whole time she'd been connecting with Beatrice. On her paper was the great blue whale traveling through space, surrounded by stars, energy, and swirls of colors. She set the sketchbook on her nightstand and stared at it as she drifted off to sleep, to dream of flying through space and time to meet Beatrice in another dimension one day.

-Cordelia McKenna

16

To Soar

When Cordelia arrived at the pier later that evening, the sky was filled with swirling swatches of pinks, purples, and blues. It looked just like the waves of energy Cordelia had been imagining all afternoon.

She sat cross-legged at the end of the pier to wait for the darkness to finally set in as the sun put itself to bed.

What else is out there? Who else is out there?

In just one afternoon, Cordelia had found so much new comfort and excitement about life. She was buzzing with energy and anticipation for what Beatrice would teach her tonight.

A mosquito's bite on her ankle snapped her out of her thoughts and she saw it was now quite dark. An almost full moon provided lots of light and created the illusion of sparks and sparkles bouncing on the swells. Everything seemed to be so much...*more* now.

Just then, Beatrice rose gently out of the water. Her giant eye peered at Cordelia. "Hello, Child. I hope you rested. You've much to do tonight!"

"I can hardly wait! I did nap. I had a dream about meeting you in another dimension."

"That sounds lovely. It will happen one day, no doubt. But no time for talk of dreams. Let's begin. Yesterday you connected perfectly and quite naturally to the universal energy field when you floated. I want you to do that again, but this time, do it with an object. What do you have with you?"

"I only brought a flashlight for the walk home. Will that work?"

"Yes, but take the batteries out. No extra energy sources. Set the flashlight on the pier, then raise it with your mind."

Cordelia took the batteries out and set the flashlight down. She stared at it as she let her mind open up. And soon she felt her mind connecting with the buzzing energy of the atoms, electrons, and protons in the flashlight. It was easier now that she had connected with Beatrice all afternoon.

The flashlight began to wobble, then to spin in a circle. Slowly at first, then a bit faster until one end lifted up off the pier and then the other end. Cordelia kept her focus. It was as if the flashlight was a part of her, and she raised it up as easily as she could lift her arm. She made the flashlight bob up and down, made it shoot ten feet in the air, twirl around, and then slowly controlled its descent until it was floating in front of her face. Then she spun it around faster and faster until it almost disappeared like the blades of a fan.

Finally, she let the flashlight hover and plucked it from of the air. "It's like I know exactly how to do that, but I don't know *how* I did that. I can't explain it."

"You're accessing the knowledge faster than I thought you would. Next, let's try to manipulate matter. It's similar to moving it, but not exactly. Find a tree and choose a branch."

Cordelia looked toward shore and picked a tall shortleaf pine just a bit back from the water's edge. She spotted a low branch set slightly apart from the others. "Okay, got it. Now what?"

"Bend the branch. Change the shape of it."

"Really? Like break it off?"

"No, no. Don't break it. Just bend it. Change it. Move the atoms of the branch and make it a different shape. You won't hurt the tree. You're not adding or taking anything away, you're just moving things around a bit. You can always ask permission if you're worried."

"Ask...permission? Of the tree?"

"You'll understand once you've connected with it."

Cordelia shrugged and took a deep breath. She concentrated on finding and connecting with the tree's energy. Then something amazing began to happen. Not only could Cordelia *feel* the energy of the tree, but she could *see* it, too! She was doing it! Connecting her energy with the tree's energy. And they began communicating only with energy. The pine glowed in a halo of red, yellow, and orange energy waves. The colors pulsed about the tree, as if the tree were breathing the colors in and out, all melting into and out of each other.

"This...this is the most incredible thing I've ever seen in my whole life," Cordelia whispered.

As Cordelia and the pine became connected, she could feel energy flowing back and forth between them like it was a conversation with no words. The soul of the pine was speaking with her, giving her permission to become a part of it. As the tree gave itself completely to Cordelia, she found she could move its branches like she could move her fingers. She was part of the tree and the tree was part of her. The branches began to sway up and down, back and forth, mimicking Cordelia's fingers. She bent the low branch, feeling a surge of atoms shift and rearrange as the branch turned upward in a gentle arc. She smiled at the tree. *Thank you.* The tree acknowledged her thanks. As they disconnected, the vibrant, dancing colors around the tree faded until they disappeared.

"Whoa," was all Cordelia could manage.

"Very good! Very, very good," Beatrice exclaimed. "That was deepest level connecting! If I didn't know better, I would swear your soul was at least at a third life energy level."

"Oh Beatrice, that was...so...I just...I can't...I get it! I felt...so...I was part of that tree, Beatrice! I was that tree... and the tree...the tree was me! And the colors...I just... Nothing could be more amazing than that—to feel so completely connected with something else."

"Just wait for what's next, Child."

"What now? What could possibly be better than that?"

"I thought it would take more sessions, but it's clear you're ready now. How do you feel? It's important you're not too tired the first time."

"I'm bursting with energy! I feel all lit up inside, like I'm glowing!" Holding her arms out wide, Cordelia began to twirl.

"You *are* glowing. Your energy waves are radiating off of you in giant, rippling colors. Look at your hands, you'll see."

Cordelia stopped spinning. She held up her hands and had to squint from the brightness emanating from them. It truly looked like her hands were engulfed in multi-color flames!

"Oh!"

"Yes! It's time. Cordelia, you're ready to fly. Go see what you're capable of."

Beatrice herself began to glow as Cordelia connected more deeply with the whale and the universal energy field. A halo of blue-green light grew around the whale, getting brighter and growing into a giant sphere. It stretched as far as the eye could see—an enormous sphere of light that glowed and moved like fire, made up of whites, blues, and greens that pulsed and melted in and out of each other. The sphere lit the depths of the ocean so brightly that Cordelia could see, for the first time, the absolute enormity of Beatrice. The whale and her energy field were breathtaking.

Their colors glowed brighter, pulsed in great bursts where their energies connected and overlapped. Somehow Cordelia could actually *feel* the colors, too. Cordelia could feel Beatrice's soul—feel the energy of all her lifetimes as their energies melded together into one.

"Beatrice," she whispered. *If all humans could see like this, really see each other's energy and light and more importantly, feel it, the world would be a far different, far more beautiful, far more peaceful place.*

"Cordelia, it's time. Fly, my Child."

And Cordelia flew.

She rose into the great sphere of energy, light, and color. She rose slowly at first, then faster and faster as she managed to control the energy waves propelling her upwards. She didn't dare close her eyes for fear of missing any of the dazzling display of colors as she flew by. She tried to memorize every detail, every sensation, as she moved. The smell of the salty air, the rushing wind against her warm skin, the waves of the ocean lapping as they rushed to meet the shore. She wanted to remember the feel of all this, should it never happen again.

She was flying.

Cordelia bent her head back, and stretched out her arms, and laughed.

"How is it *possible* we forgot all this magic? This wonderful, beautiful magic!"

She was completely one with the energy of this world—and all the other worlds Beatrice said were out there.

Cordelia flew a bit higher, then turned and swooped down towards the ocean. Suddenly out of the corner of her eye she saw a glowing light. She looked over. "Charles! It's you!"

Cordelia laughed as she connected with the pelican, and they soared together down to the water.

They flew along the surface of the water, two glowing spheres of light pulsing and dancing over the waves. Spray splashed her face. Three dolphins jumped out of the water, playing and keeping up with her and Charles. The five of them connected together in a giant sphere of swirling colors. Two more pelicans joined them and

they raced along the ocean—all of them sharing in each other's love, energy, and joy, zigging and zagging across the swelling waves.

Cordelia looked up to the moon and stars, soaring faster and faster, higher and higher.

"Go fly, dear Child. Soar!"

Moments later Cordelia shot through the colors, through the sphere of Beatrice's energy and up into the night sky. She flew faster towards the stars, feeling herself tapping into more and more universal energy. She felt as if she could fly forever—as if she could bump into one of those stars, or the moon itself if she kept going. Was the moon smiling at her, inviting her up for a visit? Yes, she was sure of it!

"Hello there, Moon," Cordelia called. "A pleasure to meet you!"

Finally, Cordelia slowed. She needed to catch her breath. She marveled at the field of twinkling diamonds the stars seemed to create. Then she looked down and gasped. There was nothing but twinkling lights below her. *Where's the ground? Have I actually flown into outer space? What's going on?"*

Cordelia began to panic. She had lost all sense of time

and space. Beatrice's calm voice filled her mind. "Take a breath, Cordelia. You're okay. Let your brain adjust and catch up. Take your time and *look*. Then *see* what you're actually looking at."

"Okay...yes. Thank you. It's all overwhelming." Cordelia took a deep breath and shut her eyes. She calmed herself, then slowly opened her eyes.

As her eyes and her perception adjusted, she located the sphere of light of Beatrice's energy field below and regained her bearings. What she had thought was a field of stars below her, she realized wasn't a field of stars at all. It was people! The people on Ananda Island! It was the shining light of people's energies, their souls—Cordelia was seeing people as they truly were. Each person was a little sphere of glowing light. They were all so beautiful, each and every one of them. Her heart filled up with love.

Cordelia flew down closer over her island to get a better look.

Light was emanating off people walking outside; some alone, some in couples, families, people walking their dogs—the dogs were glowing more brightly than the humans! Light was bursting out of windows from people settled in for the night. Each person seemed to have a unique color sphere from their own energy field—each with different combinations of colors. Some spheres were far larger than others, and one sphere was actually encompassing a whole house with a pattern and colors similar to Beatrice's. And Cordelia knew. *Of course. It's Ms. L.'s house.*

Her own house had lavender, yellow, and white lights streaming from the front of the house. *Mom and Dad!* Janey's room glowed deeply with purples, indigos, and whites. *Your energy is just as beautiful as you are, Janey.*

Cordelia didn't want to stop. She wanted to fly forever, to live up here and never come down. But she could feel herself getting tired. She began to descend towards Beatrice, trying hard to memorize as many details as she could.

And she landed gently on the pier.

"A natural. As if you were born with wings, my dear. Did you enjoy it?"

"Enjoy it? I loved it! I wish I never had to come down. It was...*everything*! I saw it. I felt it. We're all connected. All of us. I didn't know where I stopped and anything else began. It was the most...just the most beautiful thing, Beatrice. I felt...I felt like I was myself and like I was every other person, animal, plant...all of us together, all at the same time."

"Indeed."

"That's it, isn't it? That's where all the magic comes from? When we wake up, when we realize that all together we have so much more energy, so much more... magic and power when we connect our souls together? Is that it, Beatrice?"

"Simple, isn't it? Now you know. It's time. You must show others. Wake up your town. That's *your* mission, *your* purpose. In turn, once they all know, they must then teach others off the island. All humankind must be woken up so they're reminded of their magic, their connection, and their belonging to each other. That's what you've been called to do."

"Wait! I'm supposed to do *what*?" Cordelia practically yelled. "You can't be serious. I...I don't even talk to people. No one even likes me. I can't."

"Of course you can. Just like I did for you."

"Yeah, but you're a talking blue whale! Who's *not* going to pay attention to you? But me? I'm just a weird fifth grader. How am I supposed to get anyone to listen to me? Why can't you teach people? Like you taught me?"

"My purpose was to find *you*. To teach *you*. To awaken *you*. It took me 250 years to find you. I can now pass the gift on to you. You'll figure it out, Cordelia, I have no doubts. I must go now. I'm so very tired. This took more energy than I've needed to expel in years. Go home and sleep. You'll awaken refreshed and know what to do when the time comes. Good night, Child." Beatrice slipped underneath the water before Cordelia could say a word.

"But...wait! When should I come back to the pier? Beatrice?"

There was no response.

The heaviness and responsibility of Beatrice's words hung in the air. Cordelia didn't want to let the great whale down, but at the same time she didn't want to do what was being ask of her. It seemed an impossible and monumental task, one much too hard for a girl who liked to be alone. Just when she finally knew who she was and how she fit, it seemed she was now being asked to become someone different. Then she realized. She was being asked to...*change*.

Well, I'm already a really different person than I was just three days ago. If Beatrice believes I can change even more, I guess I should, too.

Cordelia had no choice but to go home. As she went up the front steps, she realized how exhausted she was.

She quietly opened the door and got to her room without anyone noticing except Kalispell, who began purring as she followed Cordelia into her bedroom.

Cordelia climbed into bed with all her clothes on. The moment her head hit the pillow, she fell into a deep, dreamless sleep.

She didn't wake up for three days.

17

Doctors and Disbelief

Though she was awake, Cordelia kept her eyes closed. She began replaying last night's adventure, wanting to remember every moment and sensation.

Cordelia smiled and stretched her arms above her head ready to soar...but something wasn't right. Something was pinching her arm. Hard. She opened her eyes and was greeted by a woman's face peering into hers.

"What the...?"

"Hello there, Cordelia. I'm Dr. Hart. Do you know where you are?" The woman's voice was soothing and pleasant, but it did nothing to calm Cordelia down.

She looked around and finally saw her family—her very worried-looking family.

"What's going on?! Am I in the hospital?"

Cordelia sat up quickly and saw an IV pinching her arm. She got dizzy and leaned back against the pillows. "What's wrong? Why am I here?"

"Take it easy, Cordelia. I'm going to need you to be still, sweetie," Dr. Hart said.

Mom rushed to the bed. "Oh, thank goodness! Oh, Cordelia, we've been so worried!"

"Cordi-Pie, am I ever happy to hear your voice!" Dad's eyes were red-rimmed and puffy. So were Janey's and Mom's. They'd been crying. But why?

She glared at Dr. Hart. "Tell me why I'm here!"

"You've been asleep for three days, Cordelia. Your parents couldn't wake you. Dr. Gabriel couldn't find anything wrong with you, but as a precaution he had your parents bring you here. I'm glad they did. An eleven-year-old girl doesn't just go into a coma-like sleep for three days."

Three days! No wonder they're upset! Cordelia tried to piece things together as quickly as she could. *Beatrice said I'd be very tired. She should have warned me I'd be in a coma! This isn't how I want to tell them what I've learned.*

★ 130 ★

Cordelia tried to connect with Beatrice. "Beatrice, can you hear me? I need your help." But there was no answer. "Please, Beatrice. I really need you!" she tried again.

"Cordelia, can you answer Dr. Hart," Mom asked.

"What? Sorry. I was thinking. What did you say?" Cordelia looked at the doctor.

"I asked what you were doing three days ago. Your parents said you'd been out late the past several nights and they thought you'd made some new friends. What did you all do? Did you take any drugs?"

"Drugs?! What? No! No way!"

"Cordi, I know you've been wanting to fit in," Janey said. "I know what some of the kids on the island are up to. Did you take something? Just tell the doctor if you did anything. We won't be mad at you, but the doctors have to know what you took. Please, Cordi!"

"What? Nothing! I swear!"

Mom, Dad, and Janey looked like they hadn't slept in three days, either. This was awful! What a mess. She had to get them to understand. Then she remembered what Beatrice had said. Her purpose! Her mission! She had to tell them!

Beatrice said she'd know when it was time. Seeing her worried family—this sure seemed like a good time to start to explain.

Cordelia took a deep breath, looked at her family and Dr. Hart, and began to talk.

She told them everything.

She described Beatrice and how she talked to the giant blue whale at the pier. She told them about the magic of energy connecting, how it meant connecting with another's soul energy, and how it allowed you to be able to communicate with just your thoughts and feelings. She described lifting the flashlight, bending the pine branch, connecting with energy waves, and flying over the ocean with the pelicans and dolphins. And then, finally, she told them about flying over the island, seeing all their neighbors as beautiful, glowing spheres of light.

"It's just so beautiful! And we all have these powers. It's magical when we can tap into the universal knowledge. We can all do it, all of us!" Cordelia couldn't stop. "I have so much magic. Beatrice says I have more than any human in centuries and centuries! But we all have it! And I'm here to wake you all up, help you understand. It's my purpose to show you all! It's so beautiful when you tap into it, I can't wait for you to try. It's hard at first, but once you make this tiny shift, just in your mind, it all makes sense! Just wait until you try! You'll see!"

No one said a word. The only sound was the hum of medical equipment. They all just stared at her. Dad's eyes brimmed with tears. "Oh...Cordi..."

"What? You don't believe me? Have I ever lied to you? Have I ever made anything up, *ever*? Why would I make this up? Here! Let me show you!"

Cordelia swung her legs out from under the blanket and put her feet on the floor. She swayed with dizziness.

"Cordelia! Get back into bed," Mom demanded.

"Cordelia," Dr. Hart said in her soothing voice, "you've had an IV in and haven't had solid food in days. You're weak."

Cordelia put her hand on the edge of the bed until the dizziness passed. "It's okay, trust me! Just let me show you." Then she laughed. "Really, I promise, it's okay!"

Cordelia closed her eyes, shifted her mind. She waited for the little prickles of electricity.

But nothing happened. *This has got to work! What's wrong? Oh, man, now's not the time! Please work!*

Cordelia tried connecting with Beatrice again. *Beatrice! Where are you? Help me! I need to show them I can fly or they're gonna think I'm doing drugs or I'm crazy or something!*

But there was no reply. Just more silence and concerned, sad looks from everyone in the room. Janey looked away, but Cordelia heard her sob.

"Cordelia, what are you doing?" Dr. Hart asked.

"Beatrice! Beatrice where are you?" Cordelia called out. "Please answer me! Help me! You said I was supposed to show them! But you're making me look crazy and weird like everybody thinks I am!"

"How long have you been hearing voices, Cordelia?"

"What? No! It's not like that! It's not! Beatrice is real! She taught me how to fly! You have to believe me! Daddy! You have to believe me! It's true!"

Dad smiled at Cordelia, but she saw he was heartbroken.

That's when Cordelia saw what her family saw, heard what her family heard: An odd, eleven-year old girl standing in a hospital room swearing she could talk to a magical blue whale who had taught her how to fly. *If I can't make my own family believe me...* Cordelia's face was hot and her chest tightened as she willed a flood of tears not to fall.

"I have something to tell you," Janey said to Dr. Hart. "Something I heard."

Cordelia looked over at Janey, suddenly remembering the other morning. "Janey. Please. Don't."

"It's for your own good, Squirt. I have to tell them." Janey turned to the doctor. "I heard Cordelia talking to someone four days ago. She didn't realize I was home. She was having this whole conversation by herself. I was listening for longer than she knew. I... I should have said something earlier!" Janey started to cry.

"Stop it! It's true! I can fly," Cordelia yelled.

Mom looked from Janey to Cordelia. "Oh my sweet, sweet girl. Hush now. People can't fly. It's just not possible."

"You know it's not possible, Cordi," Dad said. "You love science. You understand facts and figures more than most people. Everything you're saying, it just...it just can't be true."

Dr. Hart took charge of the room. "Okay, let's not all overreact." She looked at Cordelia. "Kids have vivid imaginations. Let's run a few tests. See what's going on." The doctor's voice was gentle, but Cordelia knew she thought something *was* wrong with her. Cordelia knew that once they were all out in the hallway, Dr. Hart would tell Mom and Dad she was crazy or something was wrong with her brain—that she was sick. Very sick.

Cordelia felt completely betrayed. Defeated. And worst of all, the people she loved and trusted most in the world were making her feel as weird as everyone always said she was.

Something inside Cordelia seemed to break in that moment.

"Cordelia, let's get you some food, okay," Dr. Hart said with that same fake voice.

Cordelia lay down with a brokenness that seemed to seep into every inch of her body.

Why did Beatrice tell me to do this? Why is Beatrice not helping me when I need her help the most? I trusted her—and she's just left me all alone in this room, looking and sounding...crazy.

Cordelia put her face into her hands and began to weep. She sobbed until her whole body was wracked with sadness.

Mom rushed to hug her. "Oh Cordi, it's okay. It's okay. We'll figure this all out. I promise." She held Cordelia until her sobs slowed and were replaced with hiccups and sniffles.

How was she supposed to show the rest of the island what she needed to, if she couldn't even show her family?

She was angry at Mom for not believing her, but she also wanted, needed, to feel that comforting embrace. Cordelia sank into her Mom's arms and thought about what she could say to convince everyone she was telling the truth.

But then Cordelia had a terrifying thought. *What if I am crazy? What if none of this is true and they're all telling the truth? What if I made all of this up?*

18

All the Gray

"Why don't we all give Cordelia some space," Dr. Hart said. "I'll have the nurses bring in some food. Are you hungry, Cordelia?"

Cordelia's stomach growled. "I'm starving. Yes, I'd like to eat," she replied flatly.

"Very good! Family members, let's go out in the hall. We need to get some papers signed for a few tests and to go over a few things, okay?"

They want to compare notes on just how crazy they all think I am.

"We'll be right outside the door if you need us, Cordi-Pie," Dad said. "Okay?"

"Love you, Squirt," Janey said. Cordelia wanted to forgive Janey. She really did. She understood why Janey said what she had, but Cordelia was still too angry, still hurting too much to tell her sister it was okay—or at least that it would be. Eventually she'd tell her. But not now.

Cordelia looked out the window as they left, noticing it was raining and foggy. The door closed with a click.

She lay there thinking about everything that had happened in just a week. It all felt so...real. How could this all just be in her mind? But logically, she knew it couldn't be. She was in a hospital bed. She had slept for three days. *What was more likely? That I'm sick, having some kind of mental breakdown, and my mind is playing tricks on me, or that I can actually talk to animals, move matter, and fly?*

The answer was painfully clear. No matter how much she wished the events of the past week to be true, it just couldn't be. Looking at the faces of the ones who loved her the most in the world, she had to accept it. They weren't betraying her; they weren't making fun of her. They were, she defeatedly concluded, telling her the truth. And she believed them.

Cordelia had, somehow, fabricated a whole fantastical world in which she could talk to a magical blue whale, connect with energy waves, and soar and dive through the night sky.

Staring out the hospital window, Cordelia's world was drained of all the joy, love, and color she had felt so deeply just three nights ago. Tears ran down her cheeks. The world was gray—from the inside out.

19

Visitor

Cordelia was eating her lackluster hospital lunch with more enthusiasm than it deserved, but as sad as she was, she was ravenous. She was just about finished with the slightly stale ham and cheese sandwich when she heard a voice.

"Hello, Cordelia."

For a brief moment she thought it might be Beatrice connecting with her. But no, it was only her neighbor, Ms. L.

"Oh dear. I came to cheer you up and one look at me and you look as if you might cry." Ms. L. laughed her giant, belly laugh. "Whatever is so wrong that you look as you have lost all hope in the world?"

"I'm sorry, Ms. L.," Cordelia said. "It's not you. I just thought you were...Never mind. I'm very happy to see you. Why are you here?"

"To visit you, silly! Your parents asked me to feed Kalispell and told me what was going on."

"Oh, right. I guess I'm sick. Or my brain is broken or something. They're going to do tests to try to figure it out."

"Figure what out?"

Cordelia stared down at her lunch tray, then said, "Nothing. Just my weird, odd brain making up stories that make me seem even weirder and stranger."

"Stories, hmm? May I hear them?

"Why? I made them up. They're not true. I know that now."

"Well, I do like a good story." Ms. L. pulled up a chair next to the bed and patted Cordelia's leg. "Go on, tell me your story, Child."

Ms. L. called her "child" in just the way Beatrice did. Cordelia stifled a sob. She missed the giant blue whale desperately. But how could she miss a figment of her imagination? It was all so confusing. And heartbreaking. How could she feel so much pain missing something that never existed to begin with?

"It's crazy. All made up," Cordelia whispered.

"Aren't those the best kinds of stories?" Ms. L. said. "Go on."

What did she have to lose now? She took a deep breath, trying to summon some invisible strength she did not feel, and Cordelia retold in detail, the unbelievable story to Ms. L. that she had told her family and Dr. Hart.

Ms. L. listened to every word without taking her eyes off Cordelia.

"Told you it was crazy. And now they're going to do tests on my weird brain, and my family is worried, and Mom and Dad must have had to close the store at the busiest time of the year." Tears welled up in her eyes. "It's all a big mess. Just like me."

Ms. L. cleared her throat. "Why, it's a *glorious* story, my dear. I believe it might be the best story I've ever heard."

Cordelia looked up from her tray to see Ms. L.'s brightly painted lips in a wide smile. "And why ever do you doubt it's true, Cordelia?"

"Did you *hear* me? I said I flew! I talked to a magical blue whale! I moved tree limbs with my mind! It's all ridiculous and impossible!" Cordelia slammed her fist on the table, knocking a container of chocolate pudding onto the floor.

Ms. L. picked up the pudding and set it back on the tray. "What *proof* have you that it *isn't* true?"

"Because none of it makes any sense. People can't fly. People can't talk to animals. People can't move things with their minds, Ms. L."

"Oh? Is that so? Have you been back to the pier? Have you gone to look at the tree branch? Have you tried talking to Beatrice? How are you so sure you're wrong and everyone else is right?" Ms. L. was looking Cordelia directly in the eye.

Cordelia felt the hairs raise on her arms as a slight feeling of static electricity rushed through her. Ms. L. kept her gaze steady. Cordelia held the elderly woman's gaze, but then shook her head to snap herself out of it. "I tried! I did! I tried to talk to Beatrice, I tried to fly in front of my parents and Janey and the doctor. I looked just as crazy as they thought I was! I'm weird...and now I'm crazy too!"

Ms. L. acted as if she hadn't heard a word Cordelia had just said. "You said you were tired after your meetings with Beatrice. You needed to eat and rest to restore your energy. Well, you seem to have the rest part covered having slept for three days. Maybe you should finish your lunch." Ms. L. stood up.

"Ms. L., now you sound just as crazy as I do. I'm pretty sure," Cordelia picked up the pudding, "chocolate pudding isn't going to give me magical flying powers."

"Maybe, maybe not. I suppose it depends on what it is you choose to believe."

"You can't just choose what's real and what's not, Ms. L. You can't make up stuff and make it true just by believing it. Facts are facts. And it's a fact that I'm weird. And I believe I made up a weird story that isn't true."

It was getting dark out now. The pale gray of the day was fading to black.

Ms. L. walked to the door. "I must go now, Child, I'm quite old, you know, I tire easily these days."

Cordelia gasped.

"Beatrice?! Ms. L.?!"

But she was gone.

20
Realization

Could Beatrice and Ms. L. somehow be related?

Cordelia looked at the clock. She didn't have much time. They'd be here to take her for tests soon.

She pressed the call button for the nurse. A moment later a nurse walked in. "Yes, sweetie? Everything okay?"

Cordelia picked up her pudding container. "Can I please get more food? I'm still so hungry!"

"Of course. Dr. Hart will be happy to hear you've got such a good appetite. I'll have another tray sent right in."

"Thank you!" Cordelia smiled for the first time all day. She had an idea.

This will work. It has to.

21

Belief

Another lunch and two pudding cups later, Cordelia was full. Almost uncomfortably so.

She patted her belly. *That should do it! I hope I don't get air sick.* She giggled at her terrible joke.

Why had she not realized earlier? She couldn't summon Beatrice with her thoughts, much less fly, because she hadn't eaten in three days. She was weak. She was so caught up in proving her story was true she hadn't realized she just didn't have the energy.

She quieted her mind and began to focus on Beatrice. She imagined her energy waves of white, blue, and green. She imagined connecting with them, merging her own energy with the whale's. Then in her mind she asked, "Beatrice? Are you there? Can you hear me?"

Silence. Cordelia took a breath and tried again. This had to work!

"Beatrice. Please. I need to talk to you. Where are you?" Cordelia concentrated harder.

Still nothing.

Cordelia quieted her mind even more. Focused more intently, willed herself to connect Beatrice's mind with hers. "Please, Beatrice. Connect with me! I need you."

Absolutely nothing. Cordelia opened her eyes. How could this be? She was so sure, so sure she would hear Beatrice's voice. She was rested, she had eaten, what else could she do? Defeated, she lay down and let the tears come with the final realization that none of it was true.

But wait! What was it Ms. L. had said? "I suppose it depends on what you choose to believe."

Cordelia sat up and wiped away her tears. She pushed the blankets away and stood up, steady on her feet.

"I let them make me doubt myself," she said out loud. "I wasn't *believing* what I know is true. I know it's true. I *believe* it's true."

She remembered the power Beatrice said words had and added, "I *can* do this."

Cordelia closed her eyes. This time she imagined being on the pier, remembering the first time she had lifted herself up with a mere shift of her mind. No doubts, no wondering, she just *knew*. Cordelia entered into that same state of consciousness, and the truth, *her truth*, what she *believed in*, seemed to fill every cell in her body. She opened her eyes.

Her head was brushing the ceiling. "Yes! Finally! I knew I could do it!"

"There you are, Child. I've been waiting for you. What took you so long?" Beatrice's soothing voiced filled Cordelia's heart.

"Oh, Beatrice, I doubted myself. I doubted you, I doubted it all! I'm so sorry!"

"You found your way back. I knew you would. You may have had doubts, but I never did."

Just then Janey walked in the room.

"What the...Cordelia?!" she shrieked.

Cordelia dropped quickly to the floor.

"Janey! Shhh! Close the door! Come here!"

Janey, robot-like, shut the door and peered at Cordelia. "What—"

"Janey, you *have* to listen to me. It's true! Everything I said is true!"

"But...I don't understand. What...You were...in the... air...How?" Janey stammered.

I know it's a lot, I get it. But I don't have much time. You have to get me out of here. Once they start testing me, who knows what will happen! Will you help me Janey? JANEY!" Cordelia had to yell to snap her sister out of her stupor.

"Cordelia? How...How were you doing that?" Janey sounded scared now.

"I'll explain on the way. We need to get to Ms. L.'s house. She'll know what to do." Cordelia had no idea why she said that, but as soon as she did, she knew it was exactly the right thing to do.

"Yes, Ms. L. can help. She knows." Beatrice's words filled her mind.

"Thanks, Beatrice," Cordelia said out loud.

"You're talking...to her...right now...Aren't you? You're talking to the whale?"

"Janey, you love me. You know I'm weird, and I am. But I'm not lying and I'm not crazy. Please just trust me and help get me out of here. I need you to trust me and do this."

Janey shook her head. "But Mom and Dad. The doctors. Everything they said makes a lot of sense. You should let them do the tests."

"Janey, you just saw me floating in the air! You can't deny that. You saw me! I can prove what I'm saying if you just get me out of here without anyone seeing. Janey, please. Help me!"

And there it was. That look in Janey's eyes that meant she'd help her. It was the same look Janey had when she let Cordelia into McKenna's back door. "Well, you better get dressed unless you want the whole world to see you in your unicorn pjs. Weirdo."

Cordelia hugged her sister. "Thank you, Janey."

"Come on, Squirt. Let's go."

22

Escape

As they left the hospital, Cordelia felt like she was playing secret agent with Janey as they'd done back when they still played make-believe. Janey was walking ahead down the hospital hallway, making sure the coast was clear, then looking back and giving Cordelia a thumb's up to run down the hall to meet her.

They tried to stifle laughs and giggles as they made their way down the halls.

They had one close call when a security guard stopped them on the first floor just a few feet from the exit. "Hey, girls, what are you doing? This isn't a place to play. There's a lot of sick people here. Not everybody has a reason to smile. Show some respect."

"You're right. Sorry," Cordelia said. Mom and Dad thought she was one of those sick people. They must be so worried. She had to hurry.

The guard softened. "Oh hey, I didn't mean to make you feel bad, kid. Keep smiling! I'm just being a grumpy old man. Go on now," he said and gently tousled her red curls.

At his touch, a scene flashed into Cordelia's mind of the guard in a hospital room tucking his little girl into bed.

"Sleep, Ruby. Sleep, baby girl. I'll be here when you wake up. Papa loves you." The guard watched his little girl drift off to sleep.

Ruby never woke up again. Cordelia knew this because she could sense Ruby next to her right now, could feel and see all her buzzing and glowing energy—a swirling, pulsating sphere of pinks, whites, and purples. The soul energy of Ruby's sphere connected with Cordelia. "Tell Papa I love him, please. It will make him feel better."

Cordelia wrapped her arms around the guard in a big, bear hug.

"Whoa. What's this for?" the guard asked.

"Ruby says she loves you."

The guard pulled away and looked at Cordelia. "How do you know my little girl, Ruby? Who told you to say that?" His eyes were filling with tears.

"She did. She's standing right next to you. She's beautiful. You should see her colors!"

"Janey! Cordelia! What on earth are you two doing?! We've been looking all over for you!" Mom yelled from across the lobby.

"Uh-oh!" Cordelia let go of the guard. "I have to go! But really, Ruby is okay, she never left, she's still here. Just not like how you think!"

"What in the *world*, Cordelia?!" Janey said.

Cordelia grabbed Janey's hand. "Come on! I'll explain later! We gotta run!"

The girls sprinted into the night.

"Where are we going?" Janey asked as they ran through the parking lot. "And how did you know he had a little girl?"

"I don't know, I just did. It's part of the magic." Cordelia said breathlessly. "Just keep running!"

"You have...a lot...of explaining...to do, little sister," Janey said between gulps of air.

They were out of the hospital parking lot and headed down a side street. Finally, Cordelia saw what she needed.

★ 159 ★

An empty lot with no street lights.

"This way!" Cordelia ran.

"What are we doing here? Cordelia, there's nothing here!" Janey said. "We can't run all they way to Ms. L.'s house!"

"Just trust me!"

"Cordelia! We're going to run right into that fence! Watch out!" Janey yelled.

But at that moment, Cordelia connected with the universal energy field, felt the familiar buzzing and cloud of static electricity surround her and Janey, and they lifted off the ground.

Clutching each other's hands, the girls soared up over the fence, rising higher and higher, their feet brushing the highest limbs of trees as they flew by. Wanting to get up high enough to not be noticed, Cordelia willed them higher still.

"Cordelia! I'm scared!" Janey screamed.

"I won't let anything bad happen. We're safe, I promise, Janey."

Janey squeezed Cordelia's hand tighter.

Cordelia closed her eyes, letting the connection to the universal energy wash over her and Janey, through them. She opened her eyes and saw all the swirling colors of the energy around them.

She looked over at Janey. Tears were streaming down her face. "I told you it was all true."

"Oh, Cordi, it's...it's so beautiful" Janey whispered.

"I know! Can you feel it, Janey? Do you feel the energy?"

"I feel...like this is the first moment I have really ever, truly been alive! It's amazing! *You're* amazing! Thank you for not listening to anyone else, Cordi. Thank you for trusting and believing what you knew was true!"

"Trust in it too, Janey." Cordelia started to loosen her grip on Janey's hand.

"Stop! No! I'll fall!" Janey shrieked.

"You'll be fine. I promise! You're flying right now, Janey. We're soaring on energy waves that we've connected to. You don't have to understand it. You just have to choose to believe it. Know it. Trust it. That's all you need to do. Choose to believe it's true."

Little by little, Cordelia let go of Janey's hand until their pinkies were barely touching. "Okay, here I go!" Janey yelled and moved her hand away.

"Yes!" Cordelia cheered.

The girls soared above the trees, two laughing, giggling spheres of swirling light heading towards Ms. L.'s house and the ocean.

"Am I dreaming?" Janey asked after a few minutes.

"Life is so much better than a dream. You just have to know how to think about it."

Cordelia led them to the top of Ms. L.'s cottage. "Look how it's glowing!" Janey said.

Whites, blues, and greens were shooting from the windows like spokes of a wheel. "It's because she knows." Cordelia said. "She has so much magic, as much as Beatrice, I bet. She knows about all of this. It's why I know she can help."

Cordelia grabbed Janey's hand and lowered them slowly to the ground. Janey's knees buckled when her feet hit the ground right in front of Ms. L.'s front steps.

"Oh. Woah. That was incredible! I'm so tired, now. My whole body feels like lead."

Cordelia helped her sister up. "I know you're tired, this took a lot of energy, but you're an athlete. You can do this. Dig deep and find the energy. I need you to stay with me. We still have lots to do tonight."

"Okay. I've got your back, Squirt. Whatever you need."

Cordelia smiled at her sister. "You've never let me down, Janey. Even when it hurt, you've done what you thought was best for me. I love you so much for that."

"I was just trying to help. I'd never betray you, Cordi, you know that right? It's just that I was so scared—"

"I know, Janey. It's okay. Now, come on, Ms. L. has been waiting for us."

As the girls walked up to the porch, the front door opened, blinding them with bright rays of blue, green, and white lights.

They squinted and shaded their eyes. "Ms. L.? Where are you?" Cordelia called.

The rays of light began to shorten and fade, flickering and shrinking down into a smaller and smaller sphere of light until at last it faded revealing Ms. L. before them.

"Hello, girls. I've been expecting you. Come in."

23

Fuel and Explanations

Moments later, the girls found themselves eating cookies and drinking lemonade at Ms. L.'s kitchen table.

"Thank you," Janey said. "I'm starving!"

"I'm sure you are," Ms. L. said. "You've had quite an experience tonight. You'll need the sugary boost of energy for the next several hours. It's important you maintain your energy. I'll pack cookies for when we leave. But eat now."

"Uf newf ift!" Cordelia said, her mouth stuffed with possibly the best lemon iced sugar cookie she could ever remember eating.

"Cordelia, don't be rude," said Ms. L.

Cordelia hurriedly swallowed and wiped her mouth,

noticing her napkin was embroidered with whales. "I *knew* it! You are just like Beatrice! How many times have you come back? Have you always come back as a human? Didn't you want to be a whale or maybe a bird? How old are you? What vortex did you come through to get here? What powers do you have?"

"What on earth are you talking about, Cordelia?" Janey looked dazed.

Ms. L. laughed loudly. "Yes, I know all about Beatrice. We've known each other across many lifetimes now. I came back as a human to help find you. I have to say, this life I've had has been a most remarkable one, but I'll be very happy to shed this old creaky body when I'm done!"

Cordelia swallowed hard. "You came back...for *me*? You chose to come back as a human just...for me? And you and Beatrice...You're *friends*?"

"Very good friends, Child—the best. We met over 500 years ago and decided to work together when she accepted the mission to look for you. We had no idea how long it would take. Imagine my relief when she told me eleven years ago she felt the most promising of energies coming from Ananda Island. I retired and moved here within months of her finding you."

"Mission? Looking for Cordelia?" Janey squeaked. "What are you two talking about?"

"I know this is confusing for you, Janey. Quite a lot to take in. Cordelia, why don't you explain to your sister what's going on?" Ms. L. looked at her watch. "We have some time."

Janey looked even more confused. "Time for what? Cordi, please tell me what's going on!"

"Okay." Cordelia set her cookie down. "Remember everything I told you about having magic? It's how I access the universal energy and can fly and see that guard's daughter and stuff. A long time ago, humans used the magic and could access the universal energy all the time—"

"What happened?" Janey asked. "And why do you have magic and I don't?"

"You do! We all just forgot how to access it! We all have these incredible powers! You felt it when we were flying, didn't you? When we connect to each other, it's easier to remember how to connect with the universal energy, right, Ms. L.?"

"Yes, yes exactly. Because the universal energy is *us – all of us*. It's always there waiting to be tapped into. And you figured out the key to using your magic to access it earlier, Cordelia. Brava!" Ms. L. clapped her hands.

"Wait...What's the key?" Janey asked.

Cordelia smiled. "It only works if you *believe* it works, and you also have to believe in *yourself* most of all. Beatrice and Ms. L. came here to help me do that."

"Okay...But why *you*?"

"I don't know, but," Cordelia looked at Ms. L. "I'm really glad it *was* me."

"As am I!" Ms. L. held up her lemonade and toasted Cordelia's cookie. "Now! It's time, girls! To the pier! It's going to be a magnificent show tonight!"

"The pier? What for?" Janey asked.

"It's where the town will show up," Cordelia said. "It's time to introduce this island to a talking magical blue whale! Let's go!"

"But the vortexes? The dimensions?"

"Another explanation for another time, dear. Let's go!" Ms. L. stood up.

They walked out onto the porch. "Should we drive?" Janey asked. "It'll save time."

"Drive?" Ms. L. clasped Janey's and Cordelia's hands. "Driving's too slow. We shall fly, of course!" The three of them began to glow and shine and rise into the air.

"But what if someone sees us?" Janey sounded scared.

"That's the whole point," Cordelia said. "We *want* them to see us! It's time for me to wake this island up!"

"Indeed it is, Cordelia. Indeed, it is." Ms. L. gave Cordelia's hand an extra squeeze.

They flew toward the pier.

24

The Town

Sure enough, people did see them. To the townspeople it looked as if a burst of light was traveling across the sky, like a mini comet. The phones at the police department began ringing like crazy as islanders reported the strange glowing lights in the sky. People were alarmed, but they were also mesmerized and they began walking in the direction of the lights, not really sure what they were doing but trusting some inner pull directing them to follow the glowing spheres.

Cordelia delighted at seeing all the people pointing and smiling up at the lights they did not yet understand. It was time, and it was almost her moment to shine for them all.

As they approached the pier, Cordelia saw police cars, ambulances, and several other cars parked at the clearing at the head of the path. This is where Mom and Dad would go to try to find her—and it seemed they had brought half the island with them while the other half appeared to be on their way.

As they cleared the trees, Cordelia, Janey, and Ms. L. saw Mom and Dad, along with officers, and neighbors who had volunteered to help clustered on the shore.

"Should we go down?" Cordelia asked.

"No, not yet," Ms. L. said. "Let's stay up here like a beacon, let the island have time to get here. The more people who come to see, the better."

"Look! There's Mom and Dad!" Janey exclaimed. "They see us! They're pointing at us!"

"They see our energy waves!" Cordelia said. They don't know it's us yet, but they will!"

High in the night sky, they hovered over the pier radiating spheres of colored lights against a backdrop of stars and a brilliant full moon. It was a truly spectacular sight and people could not stay away.

And then, just as it seemed the entire island had gathered on the shore and was filling up the pier, Cordelia heard Beatrice's voice in her head. "It's time, Child. Your time has come."

Cordelia smiled up at the moon and stars. She breathed in the warm, summer air. She was ready. "It's my time," Cordelia said. "Down we go."

As the balls of light floated down to the end of the pier, islanders watched with mouths agape, not believing what they were seeing, a little scared, but far too curious to leave. Everyone was cemented to the spot, not understanding anything except knowing somehow that what they were witnessing was...magical.

The lights from Cordelia, Janey, and Ms. L.'s energies dimmed and grew dark for a moment. Then a glow began to grow from the ocean under the end of the pier. Beatrice's energy grew brighter and brighter until it created a giant sphere of light illuminating the whole pier.

People began calling out.

"What is that?!"

"Are those people?!"

"It's...It's the McKenna girls!"

"It's Ms. L. too!"

"Janey! Cordelia!" Mom and Dad ran down the pier, the islanders transfixed by the whole scene. They swept the girls into a huge, bear hug, crying and laughing.

When they'd stopped crying and hugging and Mom and Dad were sufficiently convinced their girls were okay, the reality of what they had just witnessed took over.

"It's all true, isn't it? Everything you said?" Dad looked from Ms. L. to Janey to Cordelia.

"I told you," Cordelia said. "I was so mad you and Mom didn't believe me at first. You even made me doubt myself. But I'm glad you did. It made me remember for myself who I am and what I know is true. Until I remembered who I am and believed it with all of my heart, it wouldn't have mattered what anyone else thought I was...or wasn't."

By now the people of the island had all moved closer. At first they spoke in hushed whispers, but now they were getting louder. Then, as always happens when people witness things they don't understand, confusion and fear began to set it.

"Is this some kind of fireworks show?" someone yelled.

"Yeah, what's going on?" another called.

The crowd started to get louder, more and more uncomfortable with their confusion and lack of understanding.

Chief Edwards, head of Ananda's police department,

took control, "Yeah, what's going on? There's been no permits filed for any fireworks show, or any kind of... magic show or whatever this is. Someone better start explaining. Max? JJ?" He looked at Mom and Dad.

"Cordi, please...please tell us...tell us all...what's going on?" Dad urged.

"I think that's your cue, dear," Ms. L. whispered.

Cordelia stepped forward, her family and Ms. L. standing solidly behind her.

She breathed deeply to steady her nerves. The girl everyone thought was so strange and weird, the girl who preferred to be alone with her thoughts, happy to go unnoticed, looked out at the crowd.

"Believe, Child. You know who you are." Beatrice's whispers inside Cordelia's mind gave her strength. "It's time."

Cordelia had never felt more sure of herself, never felt more comfortable in who she was.

"My name is Cordelia...and I can fly."

25

Flight

The crowd was laughing and pointing. Some people were getting angry at what seemed like a big practical joke.

"You're so weird, Cordelia! Like always!" Stella Greggs called out. She and Margo were right there in the front row.

But she stayed calm. "My name is Cordelia and I can fly. I can do other things too. There's magic all around us. Right now, right here. And if you listen to me, I will teach you and show you how to use it."

"Sure you can," someone scoffed. "What else can you do besides fly? What other magic tricks do you know?"

"I know that you're lonely, Mr. Larry. You wish you had someone to come home to each night." Cordelia's energy connected with her neighbor. "You eat dinner alone in front of the TV. A tuna sandwich and chips.

Every night. It doesn't have to be like that. You have wonderful gifts, I can tell."

"What the heck? How do you know that? Have you been spying on people? I'll bring you up on charges!" the man said.

"What kind of sideshow scam is this? You're crazy!" Mrs. Henderson was irate.

"I'm *not* crazy," Cordelia said, connecting with the woman. "You dream about the future, Mrs. Henderson. But you're too scared to believe it. Scared because what you dream comes true."

"What...I...No...I don't. What is this? Max, JJ, what the heck is wrong with your kid?"

"She belongs in a hospital!" a woman shouted. "Something's wrong with this kid's brain!"

"She's always been a total weirdo," Margo Greggs said. "Our class has always known. This just proves it!"

Cordelia didn't waver. "My name is Cordelia. And I can FLY!"

And with those words, she began to glow. Whites, turquoises, and yellows surrounded her in a shining halo as she lifted into the night sky. At the same moment,

Beatrice's energy sphere glowed and shined even brighter from underneath the waves. Cordelia flew higher, the lights from the ocean grew brighter and bigger until the thunderous sound of rushing water filled the air, and it seemed the ocean was splitting in half just beyond the pier.

People gasped, watching in stunned silence as Beatrice breached, rising out of the water almost as high as the tree line. Cordelia soared across the sky, circled back to fly over, and connected their energies into massive bursts of color that lit up the night sky right as the great whale arched and fell back into the ocean.

This continued over and over, Beatrice seeming to burst and dance out of the water, crashing back down, then breaching again to meet Cordelia in the sky. Rays of colored lights surrounded Cordelia and the whale creating an indescribable beauty no human or creature had ever seen before.

Their magnificent show went on for several more minutes, dazzling the crowd below.

Finally, Cordelia began to feel weary and descended to the ground.

She stood before the crowd.

"My name is Cordelia...and I can fly."

26

Connection

The stunned people moved closer, unable to deny what they had witnessed with their own eyes.

"Teach me. Show me," Mr. Larry said.

Cordelia took his hand. "Do you feel it? I can. Your energy is strong, Mr. Larry. Look."

Mr. Larry's hand was glowing with a white light, softly, steadily. Tears ran down his face and he looked at the crowd. "I...feel it, I do!"

Cordelia turned to Janey and Ms. L. "Help me! You can show them too! We can all do this together!"

"Yes, yes, Child, that's exactly it. You'll all learn faster together." Beatrice said. "Connect yourselves!"

People were starting to hear Beatrice's voice too!

"Who is that?"

"Who are you?"

"It's okay!" Cordelia laughed. "Don't worry! That's my friend, Beatrice! And if you can hear her, your magic is strong!"

Ms. L. grabbed Max and JJ's hands which began to glow. Janey went into the crowd, held Mrs. Henderson's hand, and it too began to glow.

"Everybody hold hands!" Cordelia cried. "We'll all be stronger that way. I can't really explain it in words, but if we hold hands and connect, you'll begin to understand. You'll just know...you'll feel it. I promise." She kept hold of Mr. Larry's hand and gripped Mom's hand as well.

One by one, everyone—even the most skeptical ones—held hands. A chain of people was created from the pier all the way up the shoreline. And the more they opened up their minds, the more they began to believe, the stronger and stronger their powers got. Glowing rays of light emanated from the line of connected people. It was not their connection to the universal energy, but to each other, that made the magic and energy strongest of all.

Some folks discovered they had the ability to fly right away. Some started to move branches on the trees. Some

listened to Beatrice and just laughed with joy. Magical discoveries were made. People encouraged each other, telling each other to trust in themselves. The energy on the island kept getting stronger and stronger.

"Everyone keep your energy connected. Keep holding hands," Beatrice said. "There's something I need to tell all of you."

When everyone was holding hands, connected like this to Cordelia and to each other, they could all hear Beatrice's voice in their minds.

Once she had their attention, the great whale surfaced.

"You have been given a gift today. I hope you choose to believe in yourselves and each other. There's so very much you don't know. Keep learning, keep discovering, but be open to the magic around you right now. Each and every single one of you is extraordinary. Cordelia is going to keep reminding you, keep sharing with you, keep you all connected. But ultimately it's up to each of you to choose to keep your minds open to the possibilities of this world and to find the extraordinary that exists within each of you. Stay awake, I beg you. Stay awake. But most of all, stay connected—you are all more extraordinary *together*."

"You'll keep teaching me, right Beatrice? Cordelia asked. "There's so much more to learn. I have so many questions."

"Child, my mission in this world has been fulfilled. I've kept my promise to the universe. I've found you and I've passed on what I needed to teach you. The rest is for you to discover—for you all to discover...together."

"What do you mean? What are you saying?" Cordelia broke free of Mom's and Mr. Larry's hands and ran to the edge of the pier, getting down on her knees to get as close to the whale as she could.

"I'm so very tired, Child. This was my last pass through the vortex, I knew that. I've no more energy left. My time has come to leave this dimension." Beatrice's voice was weakening.

"No!" Cordelia cried, realizing what was happening. "You *can't* leave me! Please! Beatrice...Please...Don't leave me! I can't do this without you. Please..." Tears coursed down her cheeks.

"Don't cry, my dear child. We'll see each other again. You know that. I love you, my brave, magical Cordelia. You were more than I could have ever hoped for, you met and surpassed my every expectation. I've no doubt the people of this island will do the same. Stay connected. That's the secret of the universe, the key to accessing the magic in the universe. Stay connected and believe." Her voice was now barely a whisper.

"Beatrice. But...I'll miss you so much." Cordelia choked out. "Please...Don't go. Not yet."

Ms. L. kneeled down beside Cordelia, putting her hands on her back. Cordelia clung to Ms. L., overcome with grief and loss. "You're not going to go too, are you?" she asked through sobs. "I don't think I can stand it if you go, too!"

"Hush, Child, no, no. My time is far from over on this earth. You need me, this island needs me. It's why I'm here." Ms. L. softly said, rubbing Cordelia's back.

"I am going." Beatrice whispered." This mission has been my most honored privilege, Cordelia. A gift to me from the universe."

"Beatrice, I...I love you," was all Cordelia could manage between sobs.

The great whale glowed brighter as she slipped beneath the water. The islanders still holding hands, watched the whale's glow move away from the shore, fading and fading until at last the light disappeared into the depths of the ocean.

"Believe and stay connected. Stay connected..." were the last words the crowd heard Beatrice speak.

But to Cordelia alone she said, "I have loved you for eternity and will continue to do so. We are connected forever and will never truly be apart."

27

Extraordinary Possibilities

If an airplane had been flying over Ananda Island that night, passengers might have looked down to see glowing, dancing lights of energy vibrating and shining, rising up into the sky and shooting across the ocean. Perhaps mistaking it for the Aurora Borealis. They would have gasped with delight and wonder, curious about what they were seeing.

They wouldn't have realized they were witnessing the very beginning of a grand change across the planet. The beginning of a shift in the mind of humankind. A shift that would awaken a slumbering magic only accessed through our deep connection to each other. A magic revealing the extraordinary possibilities that lie within us all.

Whale. Hello there.

Bonus content! To write this story, I did lots of research about blue whales. I kind of became obsessed with how amazing they are! I became so obsessed that I have an eleven-foot-long blue whale sculpture hanging in my living room. I'm sitting under it as I write this right now! But that's another story for another time.

I discovered lots of cool facts about blue whales which I'm going to share, but I also found out about a super cool scientist named Asha de Vos! She's pretty incredible! She studies blue whales off the coast of Sri Lanka—super cool, right? She also started an organization called Oceanswell that helps her study the whales and helps do a lot of other amazing things.

Dr. de Vos started her organization to help educate the world about taking care of our oceans and all the animals in it. I thought Asha was so cool that I wrote to her and donated money to her organization and asked if she would read this book and write a foreword for me. Imagine how excited I was when she said YES!

Dr. Asha de Vos photographing and documenting blue whales off the coast of Sri Lanka.

About Asha de Vos, PH.D.

- She is obsessively passionate about sharing ocean adventures and science with everyone.

- She knew she wanted to be a Marine Biologist since she was six years old because it combined all the things she loves: science, exploration, the water.

- She had to leave Sri Lanka because she could not get a degree in marine biology there, but after all of her studies, she went back to live in and serve Sri Lanka.

- She earned a Bachelor's Degree in Marine and Environmental Biology.

- She earned a Masters Degree in Integrative Bio-sciences.

- She earned a Doctorate Degree in Marine Mammal Research and Oceanography and focused on the blue whales around her island home. (Which means she studied a whole, whole lot and knows a ton about the ocean and animals that live in it!! Impressive, right?)

- Asha launched The Sri Lankan Blue Whale Project in 2008 and has dedicated her life to studying and protecting this unique, non-migratory population of blue whales.

- Sri Lanka is a small island just south of India in the Indian Ocean.

- Asha's experience with blue whales started in 2003, when she was on a research ship tracking sperm whales near her island home of Sri Lanka.

- Asha started the first marine conservation research and education organization, Oceanswell in 2017. http://oceanswell.org

Asha's Advice for Kids

"It does not matter what you do in life, just make sure it is your own dream. Do what you love, and you'll do it well (this is what my parents told me). Take the time to explore what your dream is. It doesn't need to be decided at eighteen or twenty-one because those numbers are arbitrary. Sometimes the adventure is the most interesting part. To get to where I am, I've polished brass on boats, worked in potato fields.

My more practical advice is that challenges are things you can climb over or walk around. There's no such thing as a never-ending wall. Life is all about the story, and it's a better story if there are ups and downs."

About Oceanswell

- They think BIG! They work with innovative thinkers to help solve global ocean problems creatively.

- They MENTOR! Because Asha couldn't stay to study marine biology in Sri Lanka, she wants to help and support students in her country who dream of entering this field by mentoring and teaching them.

- They RESEARCH! They study urgent needs about the conservation of the ocean. Because of all the studying done about the Sri Lankan blue whales they have solved mysteries about blue whales that no one else had yet and can now help save them even better.

- They tell STORIES! Asha travels all across the globe telling stories about whats she's learned about the magic of the ocean to increase awareness and share her passion with others.

- They EDUCATE! They work with and educate talented students who dream of working in Marine Biology but lack the opportunity and access.

Learn more about Asha and Oceanswell

oceanswell.org
www.instagram.com/OceanswellOrg/
twitter.com/OceanswellOrg
www.facebook.com/OceanswellOrg/

Cool Facts About Blue Whales

- Their scientific name is *Balaenoptera musculus.*

- They are mammals, which means they are warm blooded animals. Mother mammals give birth to live babies which they nurse with their own milk. They also have lungs and breathe air!

- A group of blue whales is called a pod.

- A whale usually lives eighty to ninety years, but one of the oldest whales known was 110.

- They can grow as long as three school buses in a row!

- A grown blue whale can weigh up to 200 tons. (Which is as much as an entire house!)

- A baby blue whale is born weighing up to three tons and stretching to twenty-feet long.

- Blue whales are the largest animals ever known to have lived on Earth.

- Blue whales only generally eat tiny shrimplike animals called krill (though the blue whales in Sri Lanka feed on shrimp!) and in one day they can eat so much krill it would weigh as much as an African Elephant!

- Blue whales aren't really blue, they just look blue underwater. They are actually a kind of blue-gray color.

- Blue whales live in all the world's oceans.

- They sometimes travel in small pods but usually travel alone or with just one other whale.

- They usually spend summers feeding in cold polar waters then migrate towards the Equator in winters to warmer waters.

- There's a population of blue whales off the coast of Sri Lanka that is the only known pod to live somewhere year-round and not migrate at all. (These are the whales Asha studies!)

- They swim at about five miles an hour but can go as fast as twenty miles per hour.

- Blue whales are among the loudest animals on the planet and can hear each other up to 1,000 miles away.

- Whales are super important to us and to our oceans! As they dive down deep, they feed in areas where there are nutrients that are not available in surface waters. They then come up to breathe and release enormous fecal plumes (yup, whale poop!) full of nutrients good for the ocean. Tiny microscopic plants called phytoplankton that are the base of every marine food web and live at the ocean surface use these nutrients along with sunshine to photosynthesize, through which they then release oxygen into the environment—that's a big deal!

- Blue whales have very few predators. Very rarely, a pack of killer whales, or orcas, have attacked a blue whale. The number one predator of the blue whale is unfortunately, humans. They are at risk of injury and death because of the heavy travel by giant container ships that cross through the whales' migration paths, sometimes striking them. They also sometimes get entangled in nets, and their world is becoming noisier as we use the oceans more and more.

- When a blue whale dies and sinks to the ocean floor, they remove carbon from the atmosphere. By removing this carbon and bringing it into the depths of the ocean, these whales help us to delay the effects of global warming.

Where I Found My Information For This Book and About Asha

- wildnet.org /the-unorthodox-blue-whales-of-sri-lanka
- www.nationalgeographic.com/animals/mammals/b/ blue-whale/
- hub.wiley.com/community/exchanges /discover/blog/2018/03/05/women-in-research-dr-asha-de-vos
- oceanswell.org

About the Author

Michelle Nelson-Schmidt is an author, illustrator, public speaker, mother, sister, daughter, and wife. She loves dogs, the beach, and a really great Boston Cream doughnut from time to time. But most of all she loves living life enthusiastically and exuberantly while making a whole lot of mistakes along the way.

Michelle lives in Perdido Key, Florida, but travels extensively across the United States to visit as many schools and libraries as she can to talk with as many children as possible.

Michelle has written and illustrated six picture books:

Cordelia

Jonathan James and the Whatif Monster

Bob is a Unicorn

Dog and Mouse

Dogs, Dogs!

Cats, Cats!

Cordelia and the Whale is her first novel. She hopes you like it. Find out more about Michelle on her website, **www.MNScreative.com.**

Acknowledgements

I can't finish this novel without taking a moment to say thank you to the key people who helped me achieve my goal of getting this story down on paper.

Thank you, first and foremost, to my incredible editor, Emma Dryden, who took me on as a client. You made me weep with joy and relief when you said you believed in this story and that you wanted to be a part of making it a reality. Your insights were invaluable, and you made this book so much *more* magical than it ever could have been.

Thank you to my copy editor and sister from another mister, Beverly James, for your eyes and attention to detail and especially for all those dialogue tags I did wrong. I love you, Loserhead.

Thank you to my best friend in the whole wide world who has been talking me off cliffs for over twenty five years now. Melinda Mesina, I might have lost my mind had you not offered to do my cover design that day. I love you forever and ever, amen.

Thank you, Erin Marsicano, for reading this book when it was long, convoluted, and unedited to your Sophia Jane—then you read it again to help me with a final proofing. It was such an honor to have you and Sophia Jane be a part of this journey. By finishing this book, I kept my own personal promise to your daughter. I hope I made you both proud.

Also, I must thank my amazing husband, Kevin Schmidt. You put up with my outbursts, tears, crazy schedules, and ridiculous amounts of stress along with a house I didn't much clean for six months while I travelled and completed this book—along with two other books. I promise not to have another book idea for a while. Maybe. I love you. And you love me. Even if I lie about not having more book ideas.

And last, but certainly not least, 'thank you' will never do justice for all the support, cheers, funny memes, messages, texts, phone calls, and emails of support from all my friends on Storytime Live, Facebook and Instagram. I have met some of you in person, but most of you are 'virtual' friends. But no matter, you all mean more to me than you will ever know. You have kept me going when I wanted to quit, hide, run away, or just cry in a corner. You are all my people. You are my community, and I am so much more magical in this world because of my connection to each and every one of you.

You are all in my heart forever, and I sure do love you all. Love you lots.

Love, Michelle

CPSIA information can be obtained
at www.ICGtesting.com
Printed in the USA
FFHW010913030319
50749378-56152FF